# YOU SET MY SOUL ON FIRE TOO

## THE FINALE

## NIQUE LUARKS

JESSICA WATKINS PRESENTS

# SYNOPSIS

for·give
/fər'giv/
Verb

Stop feeling angry or resentful toward (someone) for an offense, flaw, or mistake.

For Erin and Tone, love has always been like juggling four knifes while standing on a beach ball, rolling 24mph down a rocky mountain. Hard times come with heartbreak, but the thrill of being in love is worth the risk. After tragedy hits, Erin and Tone from a united front and become each other's strength. They finally agree to not let the destruction caused by the past affect their present. What's a future without the one person who knows the depth of your soul anyway?

Erin decides having peace is less draining than living in resentment. Erin's unexpected selflessness makes Tone realize she's what he's been needing all along. The duo learns in love, sacrifices must be made. And though this is the finale, they are just getting started. Separate, both can be explosive at times, however, together they set an unstoppable blaze.

❀ Created with Vellum

# 1

## I MIGHT BEND A LITTLE, BUT I DON'T FOLD

### TONE

I sat still in a daze. Ma Duke refused to leave and all I wanted was to be alone. I stared straight ahead at the wall. My Ma Duke was sitting next to me talking, but I couldn't hear shit she was saying. My cousin was gone, and it was my fault.

I'd always tried my hardest to protect the women in my family because of the lifestyle I live. Deidra had been the only female cousin who treated me like a big brother. I was the first person she told when she knew deep down she liked women, and the only muthafucka she cried to when she felt like nobody accepted her. Twenty-five years old with her whole life ahead of her...and just like that my nigga was gone. Everybody that ever looked at her funny or looked at my family the wrong way had to die.

Everybody.

"Tonio." Ma Duke rubbed my arm.

I moved my arm away from her. "Ma, stop touchin' me."

She sighed. "Santonio, I know you're upset."

I stared straight ahead at the fireplace. After Dede's car exploded and her body was identified, I'd come home. Had been here for the last four hours just staring off into space. The whole day kept replaying, and I found myself asking God why I hadn't called to check on her the day before Thanksgiving. Why hadn't I picked her up to ride out with me like I usually did? My thoughts would then jump to that nigga, Bruce, calling to tell me happy holidays.

I knew he did it. I trusted my gut. I *always* trusted my intuition. Him and that nigga, Hakim were dead men walking. I knew there was a likely chance I'd get smoked too, but I was willing to slide on whoever for my bloodline. Those niggas had to pay.

Ma Duke's phone started ringing and she got up from her seat. Her heels clicked loudly as she made her way to what I was sure was the front door. I was glad her ass was leaving; all that mushy shit she had been on was beginning to irritate me. I didn't wanna be hugged, touched, or talked to. I needed space to think.

Not too soon after moms left, I heard more footsteps. They stopped for a second, and then picked back up just when I was about to get up and put Ma Duke out. I stared at the wall mural of Sanaa and Toni. I could smell her before I saw her. Her perfume relaxed me, made me hang my head. Made me feel vulnerable.

"Santonio."

I kept my head down.

"I'm sorry..." Erin squatted in front of me. She wrapped her arms around my neck and kissed my forehead. "I know how much DeDe meant to you."

Still, I kept my head low. I knew if I looked her in the eyes, I would break down.

"Your mom said she's leaving to give you some space." She stayed in a squat. "You shouldn't be alone right now."

"I'm good." My throat was dry from lack of talking, so my words came out hoarse.

"Sanaa and Toni are with Skyy." Erin sighed. "I can stay with you if you want."

I shook my head. "Nah, go home."

"San—"

"Erin, go home with my daughters."

She smacked her lips, stood up and stormed off.

I wasn't trying to hurt my baby's feelings, but I wasn't in the mood to deal with her either. I didn't want E's sympathy or her kind words. I didn't want her presence, and I damn sure wasn't in the right mental state for her kisses. I wasn't trying to make her upset. I just preferred to deal with this shit by myself. My nigga was gone.

Pulling my shirt over my head, I slouched back onto the couch. My phone started ringing and I looked down to see it was an unknown number. Laying my phone face down, I closed my eyes. I was flying out to Portland in a couple hours with my cousins. Kai Money was meeting us out there, and Gunz and Javier were already on their way.

When I heard footsteps in the hallway, I reached for my heat. Opening my eyes, I leaned forward on my knees. My house got quiet again, so I stood up and headed for the massive entry way. When I cut the corner, Erin was heading in my direction, carrying a Chanel duffel bag. I frowned.

"I had to get my overnight bag out of the car." She started up the stairs. "Roman just pulled up," she said over her shoulder.

I watched her until she got all the way to the top and disappeared. Shaking my head at her, I continued down the hallway. When I got to the tall, white and gold double doors that separated my home from the outside, I rested my forehead on one. A lone tear dropped from my right eye and I caught it before it slipped down my face. I ran both hands down my face slowly, and then punched the door.

This shit wasn't right. DeDe shouldn't have been dead. Nah, my nigga... she...

I pulled myself together and opened the door. My house sat in the very middle of the compound. Erin had her own house, and Ma Duke had her own as well, but they were both stubborn. Ma Duke claimed she wouldn't need hers until she got old, and Erin refused to even step foot in hers. Shit was about to change, though.

I stepped outside to see Ro sitting on the hood of his Benz puffing on a blunt. A double Styrofoam cup was in his other hand.

"Wassup, baby boy?" The hurt in his eyes matched mine. Even though we were all cousins, I was 'big bro.' It was my job to protect them, make sure they never went without. So, I wasn't surprised he'd showed up without an invite.

"Shit." He shrugged. "Had to get out the house for a second. Ava wanna hug all on a nigga and shit." He passed me the blunt.

I chuckled. "Shorty just lookin' out."

"Nah, she wanna nigga to cry on her shoulder." Shaking his head, he looked off. "I love her lil' crazy ass, though."

We stayed silent as we passed the weed back and forth.

"I'ma end up staying. Just riding out from here." He looked down in his cup.

I stared at him.

"I hate seeing Ava cry, so I'ma just ride out to the airport from here."

I nodded.

Roman looked up at the sky. "Ava is smart, so she'll know what to do. She loves Rajon too, so they'll be cool."

We both knew there was a great chance we wouldn't make it back alive. Chances that we knew came with the decisions we made for the lifestyle we were accustomed to living. Chances we were willing to take no matter what.

"Santonio..."

I looked toward the house at Erin.

"Sanaa wants to talk to you." She crossed her arms.

Passing the blunt back to Roman, I headed back towards the house.

"Uh...Ro, where you going?" She frowned.

He stopped halfway up the steps. "What you mean?"

"Ava said she's been calling you."

He looked off.

"Don't do my friend like that." She sighed. "At least go home and tell her you'll see her later." Her eyebrows furrowed in disappointment.

He nodded in understanding the same time I took her phone out of her hand.

"Naa-Naa?"

"Hi Daddy."

# ERIN

"You wanna talk to Mommy?" Santonio paused and then chuckled lightly. "I'ma tell Mommy you said that too." He shook his head. "Bye Naa-Naa. I love you." He tossed my phone, still chuckling.

"What she say smart?" I frowned. Sanaa had been in rare form. It was like she could sense something was wrong with her daddy.

He leaned forward on his legs, head down. "She said she mad at you 'cause you hit her."

I rolled my eyes.

"What you hittin' on my baby for?"

"I popped her. I was trying to get her out the tub and she told me *no*."

He chuckled.

"So, I unplugged the tub and we both watched the water go down the drain." I snickered. "You know your daughter still didn't get out. Gon' say 'I'm not done.'"

He sat up and looked over at me.

"So, I snatched her out and popped her hard-headed ass."

He laughed, shaking his head. "Wonder where she get that from."

I smacked my lips. "*You.*"

"Nah, love, she get that stubborn shit from you. Toni more my speed."

"Yeah, temperamental."

Santonio's hazel eyes washed over me. "Am I temperamental with you?" He licked his lips.

I shrugged. "You can be. I'm used to it."

He grimaced.

"All that really matters to me is the love you have for our daughters. They adore you. Sanaa..." I sighed. "She talks about you all day. You're like a superhero or some shit to her." Our eyes locked. "Toni says 'dada' and won't even attempt my name."

He motioned for me to come closer.

Obliging, I snuggled underneath him. "I know you're hurt, and I can relate to how you feel. When Jeanette died, I thought I was gon' lose it."

"I wanted to be there for you, but you wasn't fuckin' wit' me," he said lowly.

"I was mad at you. Mad at myself...mad at Nette."

"Why?"

"You bec—"

"Nah, why her?"

"Because of all the drama circulating around her that I was thrown into. First Kory, then Amina, and then you." I looked at him. "Nette wasn't a perfect person, but she didn't deserve to die like that."

His eyes swept away from mine, verifying what I already knew.

"DeDe didn't deserve that either, but that was the lifestyle she chose. You're not untouchable, Santonio. You think having security and big houses mean anything to people who hate your guts and want you dead?" I swiped my thumb across the burn mark on his face. "They'll do anything to hurt you and break you down by using the people they know you love."

I swallowed. Every day, I said a prayer for Sanaa and Toni. Their father was a crime lord. Every day their lives were in danger, mine too. The only reason I wasn't paranoid was because I knew Santonio would do everything in his power to keep us safe.

"This is the life *you* chose, though. So, the people that surround themselves around you know what it is." I looked down.

For so long, I tried to avoid what I already knew. Santonio was set in his ways. You either fucked with him or you didn't. If you did, you were showered with unconditional love and protection. I knew he blamed himself for Deidra's death.

"I should've killed that nigga in Portland."

"If I would've known you knew Hakim I—"

"Don't say his name in my house." His tone hardened. He then shrugged me off and stood up. "You shouldn't have been out smiling in that nigga's face in the first place."

"So now it's my fault."

"Nah, it's mine." He mugged me. "For fuckin' wit' a hoe."

I jumped up from the bed. "Say that again?" I'd come here to give him a shoulder to lean on, not lips to kiss his ass. "I'm a *what*?"

He waved me off. "Man, E, go home." He started for the bathroom.

I followed. "Santonio, if I leave this time, I done."

"Be done then," he said over his shoulder.

I stood in the doorway, arms crossed as he started the shower. "You don't mean that." I stared at the back of his head. The shiny 360-degree waves on his looked like they were spinning.

He stayed quiet.

"You're mad, so you're trying to push me away. I apologize for any part you feel like I had in this. I didn't know..." If Hakim hated Santonio so much, why was he at True's bar that day?

"Apologies don't bring dead muthafuckas back." He turned around.

"They don't!" I lost it. "But when you do, people are so supposed bow down and sweep their feelings under the rug." My fists balled up. I wanted to slug the shit out him.

His face softened.

"You probably didn't pull the trigger, but you killed Nette, Santonio." I took a step back. "I know you did it because she was going to talk to that detective. I know she was going to put you in jail because she felt bad for killing Kory. She needed someone other than herself to take the fall." Tears burned in my eyes, but I quickly blinked them back. "Your apologies won't bring her back, and I have to deal with the guilt of losing her and loving you."

*Fuck this.*

I spun around. "I'ma pray for you, Santonio. I know where your head is at, so I'ma give you the space you want." I went for my shoes.

"Erin." His sudden calmness pissed me off further.

After slipping my Uggs on, I started for my overnight bag. "Don't talk to me." I'd given Santonio more than three strikes. He wasn't exempt, hurting or not.

"Why you being dramatic?"

"Why are you being disrespectful?" We stared at one another.

He shrugged. "Cause I'ma asshole...I dunno."

I rolled my eyes and he smiled.

"You know you ain't a hoe."

"That don't mean it's okay to call me one." I adjusted my bag on my shoulder then headed for the door.

"So you leaving?"

"Did you not just tell me to go home and be done?" I kept on out the room.

He followed. "E..."

"Nah, it's cool. I'm gone."

"Man..." he drawled, wrapping his big arms around me and pulling me into his chest. "I said sorry," he whispered in my ear.

"No, you didn't." I didn't care how good his body felt against mine. Santonio was getting beside himself thinking he could talk to me any kind of way.

"My fault..." He hugged me tighter. "I'm sorry. I won't call you a hoe again." He mumbled, and I chuckled. "You forgive me?"

I shrugged. "I might if you do me favor.

"Anything."

"Go get in the shower. You stink."

He pushed me away. "You got it." Santonio started back for his room. "Come on, sucka."

## 2

# CHANGE IS INEVITABLE

ERIN

W hen I woke up the next morning, Santonio was gone. I tried calling him and he didn't answer. Before we fell asleep, he told me he was going to Portland, and I knew why. Santonio was like an active volcano; him hurting didn't compare to the anger boiling inside of him. My only fear now was him not returning.

After taking care of my hygiene, I left the compound and went home. When I pulled up, Sasha's car was parked in my driveway. Frowning, I cut the ignition. I hopped out and she opened her door. I walked past her not bothering to even look at her.

"E..." she called after me.

I ignored her.

"I know you're mad at me, but Skyy needs us right now."

I rolled my eyes as I unlocked my front door. Once I stepped inside the house, I closed the door. Skyy met me halfway down the foyer with a gloomy look in her eyes.

"What you doin' back so soon?" She took a drink from the glass in her hand.

"Santonio left, and I wanted to come check on you." I looked her over.

My best friend, just like me, did a great job at hiding her emotions. Her long bundles were pulled up into a messy bun, enhancing her already slanted eyes. Everybody said Skyy looked like she was mixed with Korean, and she did. Her mocha complexion was radiant and blemish free. She was only six months older than me, but she treated me like a baby sister instead of her best friend.

"I'm straight." She waved me off. "Skylar and Sanaa thought it was a good idea to draw on the wall, though." Skyy shook her head. "I put them all down for a nap a little while ago."

Skylar, her daughter, was five years old and bad as hell. I was sure it was her idea to draw on the wall in the first place since Sanaa knew better.

"I see it now." I chuckled as she followed me towards the back of my home. "I'ma end up putting your daughter out."

"Please do it." She laughed. "She's annoying."

I shook my head.

"Uh, E..." She sat her glass down on the counter. "I invited Sash over so y'all could nip this shit in the bud. Y'all better than that."

I stared at her, unmoved. "Is that why she's in front of my house?"

Skyy's eyes got big. "You left her out there?"

"Sure did." I took my coat off and laid it down on a stool.

"Oh my God." She rushed out of the kitchen. "You need to stop acting like that!" She called out.

*Yeah, but I'm not acting.*

I went into the cabinets and started removing everything I needed to make chicken alfredo. I didn't wanna talk to Sasha. I didn't want her at my house, or around me. I was cool on her dramatic ass. My back was to them when they entered.

"Erin," Skyy huffed.

I went for the refrigerator. "What's up?"

"Sasha has something she wants to say to you."

"I don't care." I removed the two packs of chicken I asked Skyy to take out of the freezer last night.

"Well...I do."

"Aw...okay." I stood in front of the sink.

"Sash, you want something to drink?" Skyy offered and I smacked my lips.

"Yeah, hook me up."

I spun around. "Don't give her shit in my house." I glared at Skyy. "I don't fuck with her." My eyes rolled over to Sasha. "At all."

Skyy ignored me and continued making Sasha a drink.

"Erin, I didn't come here to fight with you." Sasha stared back at me.

"Today?" I smirked. Cause if my memory served me right, she'd come to my home not too long ago on a different type of time. What was different about today? Was it because Skyy was here?

"I was wrong, E." She sighed.

Skyy sat a glass down in front of her.

"Okay." I shrugged. "You could've said that over the phone."

Her face hardened. "I'm not about to sit here and let you talk crazy to me."

"Then leave."

"Okay...hold up." Skyy jumped in to play mediator. "Can y'all both just chill for a second?" Her pleading eyes landed on me, begging me to be nice.

But I couldn't do it. I couldn't sit and act like Sasha hadn't hurt my feelings. She'd disrespected me way too many times in the last couple of months. No matter how mad Sasha had ever made me, I'd never tried to pull up and fight her. Then her blaming me for Nette's death was still on my conscience.

I turned back around and continued meal prepping.

"Erin, I shouldn't have put you in the middle of what me and Eli have going on," Sasha started. "I just do everything in my power to make us work and he—"

I spun back around. "Sasha, shut up!" Deidra was dead and she was whining about Eli. I didn't give a fuck about him or her.

My child's father was gone on a possible death mission, and Skyy was hurting even though she was acting like she wasn't bothered. Deidra had been her first and only girlfriend. They'd planned a future together and had something special up until she found out

Deidra's daddy was also Skylar's. She wasn't wearing her emotions on her sleeves, but her puffy eyes were a dead giveaway that she had been crying. She'd probably been drinking since she found out too.

Skyy sat down. "Erin, I know you're mad, but we need each other right now." She looked down into her glass. "I'm..." She paused and took a deep breath. "I haven't told Skylar yet, and I don't know how."

Facing the sink again, I washed my hands. After turning the faucet off, I stared at the granite wall.

"I'm so sad, y'all." Skyy sniffled, making me look at her.

The tears streaming down her face slowed my breathing. Sasha got up from her seat and went to her.

"I just can't believe she's gone." She looked down in disbelief. "I just talked to her the other day."

Skyy and Deidra's relationship had been all over the place the last three years. They had a love slash hate relationship once Skyy started messing with Que. Skyy didn't know Que and Deidra had been acquainted when she and Que became an item, but by the time she found out, she was already head over heels for him. Now she and Que weren't even together because he claimed he wasn't ready to love her. She respected his honesty and they stopped dealing with each other. He was the reason Skyy moved to Houston. Between Jeanette dying, finding out Deidra and Skylar shared the same father, and Que not wanting her, Skyy needed an escape from Missouri.

"I know y'all are mad at each other right now." She paused to look at me. "But our sisterhood can't crumble right now."

My eyes landed on Sasha who was already looking at me with remorseful eyes. I mugged her.

*Fuck Sasha.*

# TONE

"Ah... Santonio." Don Capporelli stood up when I entered.

I hit him with a quick reverse nod. His security stayed close to me as I made my way towards an empty seat at his dining room table. When I sat down, I noticed he was eating spaghetti and meatballs on some true Guido shit. The room fell silent when he sat back down and ate like I wasn't there. I slouched down in my seat in irritation and he finally looked at me.

"I heard about your family. My condolences."

I nodded.

"Death in a family is always tragic...no?"

I stared at him.

"This is why I have to protect my figlio."

I looked over my shoulders at both of his men. They were both toting bangers, hovering over me.

"No disrespect to the Capporelli family, but fuck your son."

He glared at me and I gave him the same look in return. Wasn't no turning back now. It was do or die, and I was ready for whatever.

With a quick wave of his hand, he dismissed his men. Don Capporelli pushed his plate away, grabbed a silk cloth, and wiped his mouth down. *"Sei come un mio figlio."*

Don Capporelli telling me I was like a son to him didn't move me. "Where is Bruce?" I didn't give a fuck about none of that.

He chuckled. "Do you know why I take to you, Santonio?"

I leaned forward on the table. "Nah, enlighten me."

Don Capporelli began twirling his pinky ringer around his finger. "You are a natural born leader. You demand respect." He stopped fuckin' with his ring but kept his eyes on mine. "Or you will take it."

"Where's Bruce?"

"Ah..." He reached over and opened the cigar box to the left of him. "Bruce..."

"Yeah...Bruce. I need to rap wit' him." I'd been in Portland two days now. The nigga was hiding from me.

"I'm not sure where my son is."

"A'ight." I pushed my chair back.

"Santonio..."

I stood up.

"I love my son."

I nodded. "Cool." I turned around and headed for the exit.

"I love him so much that I will go out of my way for his funeral services."

I stopped in my tracks and faced him.

"If you find Bruce before I do..." Don Capporelli leaned back in his seat. "Tell him, I do not tolerate dishonor." He then dismissed me with a wave of his hand.

~

"So now what?" I heard Lucus.

My eyes were closed and my head was rested on the back of the sofa.

"This nigga just gon' get away with what he did to DeDe!" he yelled.

"Fuck nah he ain't getting away with that," Drake shot back.

With my eyes still closed, I tapped my foot patiently.

"Then why the fuck we posted up instead of looking for his bitch ass." Lucus was on a rampage.

"Nigga, sit the fuck down," Roman spoke up.

"And shut up," Que co-signed.

"Y'all trippin'!" Lucus yelled. "I'ma go find that nigga by myself."

"Lucus..." I slowly opened my eyes and looked at him. "Sit down." My eyes stayed trained on him as he found a seat next to True.

"This some bullshit, dawg." He slouched over and put his face in his heads. "This shit ain't right!"

I tugged at my beard.

True, who had been quiet since finding out about Deidra, stared down at the floor.

"I swear to—"

"Lucus..." I closed my eyes.

The room went silent. He wasn't the only one mad. Every nigga on my team felt violated. There wasn't shit we could do right now, though. Bruce and that nigga Hakim were nowhere to be found. I didn't want their loved ones to fight the war they'd started, but my hands were tied.

I could get to Hakim's family before Bruce's, unfortunately. The Capporellis were technically my family too and they were damn near untouchable. Running my palm across the top of my head, I sighed. Right now, nobody was safe, on both sides. Erin and Ma Duke now had no choice but to move on the compound.

True stood up and headed for the balcony of the condo. Kai Money followed after him, and Roman left the room. Drake started making a drink and Lucus' face was still in his hands. I sat up and stared at the wall.

Pulling at my beard, thoughts of DeDe invaded my mind. She was loved by everybody, a down to earth ass chick who would go out of her way for anybody. And they'd taken her away. My nigga couldn't even have an open casket funeral because there was nothing left of her but ashes. They did my nigga bad, and destroyed my family.

Drake couldn't even talk to Aunt Paige without breaking down, so I knew Ma Duke was going through it. When I heard sniffling, I looked over at Lucus. He was the youngest. At just twenty, he'd been through a lot, but losing Deidra was too close to home for him. He was having a hard time dealing with her death, accepting what he had seen.

Drake took a seat at the bar and poured up another drink. "Tone, them niggas can't walk around like shit coo."

I nodded.

I knew he felt guilty. We all did. DeDe had been the only woman on our team besides Ava, and we'd failed her. In her last moments she'd been all alone, scared I'm sure. I looked around the room at the all the machine guns and weapons either on the floor, on tables, or at the bar. Not being able to use any of them started fuckin' with me.

We had been up almost seventy-two hours. Bruce and Hakim weren't here because they knew we were coming. I knew they weren't in Kansas City because I had the city on lock down. Nobody was moving in and out of that muthafucka without me knowing first. Deidra's death brought all the lil homies together. Hoods that had been fonkin' for years were teaming up on a manhunt.

I stood up. "Pack all this shit up," I called over my shoulder, heading to one of the spare bedrooms. "We leaving."

I made my way down the hallway with the weight of the world on my shoulders.

*I should've been there.*

# 3

## UNPREDICTABLE CIRCUMSTANCES...

ERIN

When I pulled up to the home Ava and Roman shared, I cut my car off and sat there. I hadn't heard from Santonio in almost four days. Sadee was going through it. Her niece was dead, her sister was losing it, and her only child was nowhere to be found. She insisted I drop Sanaa and Toni off with her and asked if she could keep them for a day. I knew it was so she could feel close to Santonio.

I grabbed my purse from the passenger seat and opened my door. I exited my car, shut the door and hit the lock button on my key fob. I then made my way up the walkway and to the front door. I rang the doorbell and waited for Ava to answer. Since she was expecting me, it only took her a few seconds to get to the door.

When she opened it, I immediately noticed the bags under her eyes. Ava gave me a fake half smile and made room for me to get by. After she shut and locked the door, I followed her down the long hallway and to the living room. I removed my coat as Rajon rushed to me.

"Hi, Auntie Erin." He smiled.

Tossing my coat, I pulled him into a hug. "Hey, baby." I looked around the room. "You putting up the Christmas tree?"

He nodded and I released him. "Yep, me and Ava."

Ava was now at the tree putting ornaments on it. "You talk to Tone?"

"No." I approached her. "You talk to Ro?"

She sighed sadly. "No. I've been calling him, though. Chance said she talked to True two days ago and he snapped on her. She was over here in her feelings because he said fuck her."

I grimaced. True didn't usually talk to his precious Chance like that.

"She knows he's hurting right now so she's good now."

I nodded.

"Here, kiddo." She handed Rajon a decoration. "Blaze is upset too. Kai's lawyer called her today." She looked at me sadly. "He tried to get her to sign some paperwork Kai set up and she refused."

I looked down at my feet. I didn't know Blaze all that well, but Ava spoke highly of her. I felt bad for her. She and Kai were married and just had twins not too long ago.

"You think..." Ava's shoulders dropped. "You think they're..."

I shook my head. "No, I don't."

I wanted to stay positive in all of this. Sadee was sad, Skyy was sad...and I knew Ava was too. She loved Roman, and Kai was her brother.

"I haven't talked to him in almost four days, E." Tears pooled in her eyes. "I can't..." She looked away from me and stared down at Rajon. "Kiddo, go straighten up your room, okay?"

Rajon looked up at her. "You sad, Ava?"

She smiled. "Of course not. Let me talk to Auntie Erin and then we'll finish the tree, okay?" She pulled playfully at one of his long, silky braids.

He looked at me, then back to her. "I'ma be back, okay?" He hugged her legs.

We both chuckled as he made his exit. Rajon was overprotective over Ava. It was cute because he would even check his daddy about Ava. She and Rajon had a tight knit bond that not even Leah, his mother, could break.

"This past week has been so fucked up, yo." Ava took a seat on the couch.

I silently agreed. "I'ma jus—" I stopped midsentence when my phone went off. I went over to my coat and removed it from the pocket. Hakim's name flashed across the screen and I stood still for a moment just staring at it.

"What's wrong?" Ava asked concerned.

I pressed the green icon and answered the phone. "Hello?"

"E..." His deep voice blasted. "I need to see you. It's important."

I looked at Ava. "Hakim, what did you do?"

"Man, I ain't do shit. That's why I need to see you, Erin."

Ava's eyes narrowed.

I stayed silent.

"E?" He sighed. "E, I got kids, man. I need for you to hear me out. You're the only person who can fix this shit."

"You killed an innocent woman, Hakim."

"I didn't kill her! I didn't have shit to do wit' that. That's my word. I put that on my seeds." He sounded like he was on the brink of a break down. "E, you know me. I'm a lot of things, but I'm not a scandalous nigga, man. That girl didn't do shit to me. My beef wasn't with her, it was wit' your baby daddy."

"Why are you calling me?"

"Cause I need your help, E. My family is in danger."

"I can't help you Hakim." I hung up the phone.

"What did he say?"

"He wanted me to meet up with him."

"Let's go." She headed out of the living room.

"What?" I followed her. "We're not meeting that nigga nowhere."

"Rajon!" She stood at the bottom of the staircase and yelled. "Put your shoes on!" She then spun around and went for the coat closet.

"Ava."

"Erin, look..." She sounded aggravated. "Have him send you his location and I'll take it from there." She opened the door and skimmed through her options. Finally, she removed a black hoodie. "Can you keep an eye on Rajon while I change?"

She rushed past me and headed up the stairs, taking them two at a time.

I went back into the living room and sat down on the couch. I tapped my foot, contemplating my next move. The last time I went behind Santonio's back and took matters into my own hands, it backfired on me. Massaging my forehead, I stared at the half-decorated Christmas tree. My text alert went off and I looked down at my phone.

*Hakim: E I really need your help. Please don't turn your back on me.*

Rajon ran into the room. "Where's Ava?"

I looked at him and then back down at my phone. "She's putting clothes on."

"Okay." He sat down next to me. "Where Sanaa at?"

I reread Hakim's message.

"Auntie E..."

I looked at him. "Huh?"

"Where Sanaa at?"

"With her granny." My attention went back to my phone. The three dots in a bubble let me know he was texting.

Ava entered the room. "Here, come put your coat on RJ."

My eyes landed on her and I saw that she was dressed in black skinny jeans and a black hoody. On her feet were black Timberlands and, on her head, a black New York Yankees skull cap.

"Did he send you his location?" she asked as she helped Rajon into his coat.

I looked back down at my phone. "I know where he is."

*Hakim: Please meet up with me Erin. I'm at my moms. You remember where she stays still right?*

He then sent the location.

"He's been hiding out at his moms."

I grabbed my coat and slipped it on.

"Cool. Let me drop Rajon off with his mama and I'll meet you at your house in an hour."

I nodded, passing her. "A'ight."

# TONE

10:45 pm that night...

When I entered Ma Dukes house, it was quiet. I stood in the foyer to see if I could make out which room she was in. When I heard movement upstairs, I knew she was in her room. Making my way up the stairs, I turned my fitted cap backwards. I knew she had been worried about me. I hadn't listened to any of the voicemails she had left me, but I read a couple of the texts she'd sent.

I stood in front of her bedroom door and mentally prepared for how emotional she was about to be. I then knocked twice.

"Come in," she called out.

I turned the knob and pushed the door open. When I stepped inside, I immediately noticed Sanaa and Toni asleep in her bed. Ma Duke sat in her recliner with a book in her hand. The lamp next to her gave the room a little light. When we locked eyes, a smile spread across her weary face.

"Well look who it is." She placed the book in her lap, and I saw it was a bible.

I approached her and leaned down to place a quick kiss on her forehead. "Why Sanaa and Toni here? Where's Erin?"

She shrugged. "I asked her to let me have them until tomorrow afternoon."

I nodded.

"I'm glad you're safe. Where's Roman?" Her eyes danced around me. "Is he okay?"

"Yeah, he's straight."

She smiled again and nodded. "I'm happy you both made it back safe. Deidra's funeral is Saturday." Ma Duke tried to read my body language.

I looked at Sanaa and Toni. "A'ight."

Her phone went off and she reached for it. "This is Roman right here." She answered. "Well hello, stranger."

I widened my stance and crossed my arms.

She looked up at me. "No, she's not here." She frowned. "With Leah? When?" Ma Duke paused. "Okay." She then looked to me. "Santonio, call Erin and see if Ava is with her please."

I went into my pocket for my phone. I pulled up Erin's contact information and called her. When it went to voicemail, I hung up. "What's wrong?"

"Ava dropped Rajon off with Leah earlier and now she's not answering the phone."

I called Erin back.

"He just called Erin and she didn't answer," she told Ro.

Erin's voicemail picked up again. I ended the call and went to my text messages. Clicking on our conversation thread, I sent her a text.

*Me: Call me*

"Okay, when you pick up Rajon, call me." Moms hung up the phone. "Did she text you back?"

I shook my head.

"Let me call her." She pressed on her phone a few times and then put it to her ear. A few seconds passed by and she pulled it away from her face and sighed. "Let me try Ava."

I called Ross.

"Mr. Morris?" He answered on the second ring.

"Where are you?"

"I just pulled up in front of your mother's."

"Where is Erin?"

"She should be at home. I just left there. Is everything okay?"

"Was Ava with her?"

"No."

I hung up the phone.

"Ava's not answering either."

I called Que.

"Sup?"

"You talk to Skyy?"

"Nah, she ain't answering the phone. Why, what's up?"

"Meet me at Erin's." I hung up the phone and called Roman.

"Yo?"

"Where's Chance?"

"True just got off the phone wit' her."

"Erin and them wit' her?"

"Nah. She told True she ain't talked to Ava all day. He know she lyin', though."

"A'ight." I ended the call.

"He talked to Chance?" Ma Duke was now up on her feet.

"Yeah."

"Thank God." She sighed. "So, they're all together?"

"Nah."

Her face dropped. "Well, what did Chance say?"

"I'll call you later." I started out of her room. "Ross is outside, so if you need anything just call him."

"Santonio." She followed me. "What's going on?"

"I don't know."

But I was about to find out.

～

When I got to Erin's house, Que and Roman were already there. I cut my ride off and hopped out.

"Ain't nobody here." Roman approached me.

I made my way up the walkway and to the front door. Using my key, I let us in. The lights were on, but the house was still. I headed up the stairs. When I got to Erin's room and pushed the door open, it was pitch black. I cut the light on. I looked around and noticed nothing was out of place. I took my phone out my pocket and tried calling her again. This time when her voicemail picked up, I left a message.

"Yo, Erin. Where the fuck you at? Call me back."

I wasn't one to usually panic, but not being able to get in touch with her was slowly pissin' me off.

I ended up back downstairs with Que and Roman.

"Where the fuck could they be?" Roman looked stressed.

"Call Kai Money." I started back out of the house with them following me.

# 4

## PRETTY IN PURPLE

ERIN

H akim opened the passenger door and hopped in. "Thanks for coming E. I can't trust nobody right now."

"What's going on, Hakim?" I stared at him. After going back and forth with Skyy and Ava, I agreed to meet up with Hakim. I didn't feel comfortable picking him up from his mother's, so I had him wait for me two blocks away on the corner, right up underneath the stop sign. I arrived twenty minutes early just to make sure he wasn't on nothing funny.

"Shit is fucked up, man."

"And it just got whole lot worse." Ava pressed her gun on his temple.

"You bitch!" He glared at me.

"Put your hands on the dash board and I won't shoot you." Ava gritted.

I pulled away from the curb.

"You bitches are gon' regret this." He threatened and that was all it took for Ava to tase the fuck out his neck.

Skyy, who had been in the backseat quiet, started hitting him with her gun. After a few blows to the back of his head, Hakim's body slumped against the door.

"Now what?" Skyy said from behind me.

"Yo!" Ava yelled in Hakim's face. She then shook him, but he didn't budge. He was now duct taped to a wooden chair, knocked out cold.

With my arms crossed against my chest, I paced the floor.

"Let's just shoot him." Ava smacked her lips in irritation.

"Right." Skyy agreed. "E, I get this is your boy but what he did to Deidra..." Her voice trailed off and she stormed a few feet away.

I approached Hakim slowly and stared down at him. "He said he didn't do it."

"You playin' right? Yo, Erin, you my nigga but you sound mad dumb right now." Ava pressed her gun to Hakim's forehead. "Even if he didn't do it, his ass his dying tonight." She smirked. A purple ski mask was covering her face, but the dark look in her eyes didn't go unnoticed.

I looked around the warehouse. It was pretty much empty except for about three chairs, a sink, and cleaning supplies. It was Ava's idea to come here. She'd already been here a few times with Santonio and the crew and felt like it was the perfect spot to handle Hakim. The building looked abandoned and was at least an hour away from Kansas City.

"Skyy." My eyes skipped in her direction. "Fill that bucket up with cold water.

She nodded.

Ava slid a chair in front of Hakim and sat down with her front facing the back of the chair. "His ass is fine."

I rolled my eyes at her and checked the time on my watch.

*12:49am*

"Here." Skyy came and stood next to me holding a bucket filled to the rim with water. "I put bleach in it too."

Ava laughed.

"Throw it on him."

Ava hopped up from her seat and Skyy tossed the bleach water on Hakim. His eyes popped open almost immediately. As soon as he came to, he started panicking.

"What the fuck!" Hakim's eyes bounced around in confusion. When he tried to move his arms but realized he was restrained, he looked up at us. "Erin?" His gaze shifted back and forth between Skyy, Ava, and I. "E?" he asked again trying to figure out which face hidden behind the purple ski masks was mine.

Ava, who was standing to the left of me, pointed her gun at him.

Skyy, who was on the right, held hers at her side.

"Hakim, tell me what the fuck is going on?" I mugged him. Hakim was a lot of things, but a liar wasn't one.

He grilled me. "Untie me!"

Skyy stepped forward. "Lower your fuckin' voice!"

"Yo, E... he got one more time to disrespect." Ava's gun was still pointed at Hakim. "And I'ma shoot him."

Hakim slumped back dramatically into his seat. "Erin, we better than this." He shook his head. "I didn't kill that girl."

I frowned. "But you knew Bruce would."

Hakim hung his head. "I told him to let me handle Tone's bitch a—"

Ava's gun went off and a bullet pierced Hakim's shoulder.

"Aaaaaaghh!" he screamed.

Skyy chuckled.

"I told you, you had one more—"

I pulled my gun from the small of my back. "Hakim..." I sighed. "I can't let you live."

Hakim became distraught. "Nah, E..." His sad eyes landed on mine "Erin, don't do this, man. I been knowing you forever. I got kids..."

"Fuck your family!" Skyy screamed.

"You didn't give a fuck about ours," Ava cosigned.

"I know where Bruce is."

I stared at him. "Where?"

"Let me go and I'll tell you."

Ava chuckled. "I know damn well this nigga ain't trying to call shots."

Hakim mugged her.

"Where's Bruce?" My gaze never wavered.

"I can take—"

I held my hand up. "No, tell me. Matter fact." I pulled a burner phone from my hoodie. "Call him."

"I don't know his number by heart," he stated dryly.

"Skyy..."

Skyy calmly went and stood behind Hakim. She then pressed her gun against the back of his head.

Ava retook her seat backwards in the chair.

"Hakim, I just told you I can't let you walk out of here alive." It pained me to even have to say that to a friend. I knew a huge part of me would die right along with Hakim, my first. "What I can do is make sure your family isn't harmed." If I knew Santonio, Hakim's entire family was in danger.

"E, I can leave the country," he promised.

"I'm trying to help you, Hakim." My eyes shot back and forth between Ava and Skyy. "If you give them a chance to kill you before I talk to Bruce, everybody you love is going to die."

He closed his eyes. "I don't know his number by heart, E."

"Ava..."

Ava removed his phone from her back pocket. "What's your unlock code?"

Hakim's eyes widened. "I—"

"Tell her the code to your phone," I interrupted.

"Zero, four, one, nine, two, six..." He looked down at the floor in defeat. "E, this ain't you, man."

"What's his name saved as in your phone?" I ignored him.

"B. Cappo."

I looked down at Ava.

"Got it." Ava then ran the number down for me.

I pressed send on the burner phone and put it on speaker. "Think about your family, Hakim."

With his head still low, he nodded slowly.

"Hello?"

"Bruce," Hakim said weakly.

"Hakim."

"I need to leave sooner than planned. I got niggas gunnin' after me and I ain't do shit."

I looked away.

"It's not safe to go back to Portland. Santonio is there."

"He's here too!" Bruce yelled.

"You know how many niggas he got on his payroll. Huh?!" Hakim yelled. "I'm not safe here, Bruce... I'll die."

"I am in Tivoli, Hakim. There is nothing I can do for you." Bruce ended the call.

"This nigga left the country..." Hakim said in disbelief. "I'm bouta die over a beef between him and another nigga...and this nigga left me."

We all stood silent as Hakim registered his fate.

"Don't take it personal." Ava shrugged.

Just as those words rolled off her tongue, the doors to the warehouse opened. Ross entered first, followed by True. Next came Que and Roman made his entrance soon after. My heart dropped to my stomach when Santonio swaggered in with an angry scowl on his face. His eyes were shooting daggers when they landed on me.

"Get yo ass over here!"

# TONE

When my boy Scoop called me and said three masked men walked into *my* warehouse with a body, I thought the nigga was lying. Nobody other than my team knew about this spot. When he told me the masked men on the security screen were wearing purple, I almost hung up the phone. Then I remembered I had a gangster ass business partner, a hot-headed sister in law, and a criminal minded baby mama. They were all still masked, but I knew who was who. Ava sat in the chair, Skyy was standing behind Hakim, and Erin stood in front of him, gun in hand.

"Get over here..." I said calmly this time. I watched intensely as Erin made her way to me.

"You too!" Roman called out to Ava. "You got me fucked up."

Ava smacked her lips but got up.

"Let's go." Que stepped further into the warehouse. "I know you hurt, shorty, but you can't be here."

Skyy lowered her gun and met him halfway.

Once Erin made it to me, I snatched her up by the front of her black hoodie and started out of the warehouse.

"Santonio, I told you about grabbing on me," she gritted. "Let me go."

We made it to her car with me still holding onto her. "Why the fuck you here? You ain't this dumb."

She tried to pull away from me. "I know where Bruce is."

I pushed her against the driver's door.

"He's in Tivoli."

I let her go. "Go get my daughters and go home."

"Get yo ass in the car, Ava." Roman opened the passenger door. "I'ma get wit' you when I get home. And give me that fuckin' gun!"

Erin opened her door. "Hakim's innocent."

"Why? Cause you used to fuck him?"

Erin snatched her ski mask off. "A long ass time ago!"

"Now ain't the time for this, bro." Que put Skyy in the back seat and shut the door.

E hopped in the car and slammed the door.

*I'ma fuck her up.*

I reached for the handle and she locked the doors.

She started the ignition, blasted the music, and sped off.

I exited the building thirty minutes later with my team behind me. After I put in a bullet in Hakim's head, Roman shot him in the face and Drake emptied his clip into his body. True had tried to kill him with his bare hands, and Que watched from the sidelines with a satisfied smirk. After Erin told me Bruce was in Tivoli, I didn't need Hakim alive. I didn't care that E thought he was innocent. Deidra was dead.

"I know them coming here was Ava's idea." Roman sighed. "I swear her ass get worse every day." He sounded stressed.

Que laughed. "Ava's one of us, nigga. You know Kai and them ain't raise no punk."

"She hard-headed as fuck, man."

I reached into my back pocket for my ringing phone just to see it was Brandi calling me. Pressing ignore, I continued to my route to the whip.

"Ro, ride out with True." I spoke over my shoulder. He'd rode with me out here, but I had a stop a needed to make.

When I entered Erin's bedroom, she was lying across her bed reading in nothing but a hot pink lace thong and bra. Erin was sexy as fuck. Her ink only made her that much more dope to me. I'd been trying to get her to get her ass tatted, but she complained about not being able to sit down. With the way it was currently sitting in her thong, she didn't have a choice now.

"What did I say about just walking in my house, Santonio?" She didn't even look up at me.

I pulled my shirt over my head. "Where are my daughters?"

She ignored me.

I approached her bed and slapped her hard on the ass. She winced and then looked up at me mugging. "You don't hear me talkin' to you?"

"You answered a question with a question. Plus, you weren't trying to hear shit I had to say two hours ago."

I smacked her ass again and then squeezed a handful. "Who you talkin' to?"

"*You*," she shot back.

"So, you with the shits now?" I chuckled, taking a seat on her bed.

"Leave me alone, Santonio."

I smirked. "Make me."

Erin sighed. "Your daughters aren't here, so you shouldn't be here either."

I yanked her ponytail and her head jerked back.

"Ouch!" She sat up and pushed me. "That shit hurt. I know you're not used to fuckin' with chicks that wear their own shit, but mine is real."

"Watch your mouth then."

*Smart ass.*

Erin sucked her teeth.

"This your last night staying in this house." I stared at her. "Whatever you don't get out by the end of the day tomorrow, stays." I went into my pocket, removed both of my phones, and tossed them onto the bed.

"Says who?"

"Daddy."

She rolled her eyes.

"You, moms, and the girls need to be settled in at the compound before I leave the country." My phone went off, showing Brandi was calling yet again.

Erin looked down at it and frowned.

The look on her face made me swipe my phone and answer. "Wassup?" I put her on speaker.

"I still can't believe you threw me out. I know we don't know each other that well, but I thought we had an instant connection."

Erin snatched my phone. "Well bitch, I guess you thought wrong." She then ended the call. I watched as she made herself comfortable with my phone.

Shaking my head, I laid on my back. "Yo E, let me handle my beef with other niggas, a'ight. I can't have my wife out here kidnapping niggas and holding 'em hostage."

"I brought Hakim to you, though, right?"

I looked over at her. She was still busying herself with my phone, frowning.

"We had the situation under control, believe it or not." Erin slipped her ponytail holder out of her hair.

I looked up at the ceiling. "Purple ski masks?" I chuckled.

She snickered. "Real G's wear purple."

I closed my eyes. "I ain't gon' front like that shit wasn't sexy, but where the fuck did y'all get purple masks from?"

Erin laughed. "Ava stopped and got them."

I shook my head. "Y'all wild." I looked over at my baby again. "Nah, but on a serious note, don't do no shit like that again."

"Mum hum..." she mumbled, still being nosey in my phone. "I

done blocked about twenty bitches." She stared at me. "You are ridiculous."

I chuckled. "What? I'm a single man. I get lonely."

Erin threw my phone at me and it smacked me in the face hard.

"Am I not single?"

She crawled over and climbed on top of me. Squatting in the riding position, she placed her palms on my chest. "You are." She began rotating her hips, gazing down at me all sexy. Her lips were shiny. I wanted to pull on her bottom one and suck on it. "And so am I."

I frowned and she hopped up.

"So, don't say shit when you gotta block niggas out my phone too," she snickered.

I smirked.

*Yeah, a'ight. Get you and that nigga murked.*

# 5

# YOU CANNOT BREAK DOWN WHAT CAN'T BE BROKEN

## ERIN

"I don't give a fuck about that attitude."

"*Okaaay*, Roman." Ava sucked her teeth as he walked past her and out of the door.

I chuckled. Roman was still mad about Ava taking us to the warehouse.

"Don't laugh at him, yo." Ava walked past me with a drink in her hand.

I dropped a box on the floor. "Ro big mad."

"On everything." She rolled her eyes. "I sucked his dick and everything."

"Ew." Chance entered. "That's nasty."

"I'm sure you and True know all about *nasty*." Ava smirked.

I looked at Chance and when her cheeks flushed red, I snickered. "Let me find out."

"Ain't nothing to find out." Chance stormed past us.

"Let's make a bet." Ava looked to me. "True and Chance are fuckin'."

I shrugged. "I bet they're not. But I'll bet a grand they will."

"Bet."

We slapped fives.

"E, I love you and all, but I'm not a mover." Skyy entered and kicked a box.

"Let's go have a drink." I led the way towards the back of the home Santonio had built just for me. Technically, according to him, the entire compound was mine. I'd seen the deed.

"That's what the fuck I'm talkin' about." Skyy walked next to me. "Ava's bartender!"

I nodded in agreement.

"*Nooo...*" Ava pouted. "Let Chance."

"Let Chance what?" Chance asked when we entered the kitchen.

"Make the drinks." Ava trekked towards the island and took a seat.

"With what alcohol?" Chance looked confused.

Skyy held up the two bags she'd walked into the house with. "Got it covered."

"I like her." Ava nodded.

Chance laughed, shaking her head. "Y'all do know it's not healthy to drink as much as you do? There are other ways to deal with things." She stood with her back against the counter. "And Ava, Ro already said you're done for the day."

Ava waved her off. "Roman is not my daddy. He don't run shit over here."

My eyes rolled to the kitchen entrance and they landed on Roman who was now leaning against the doorjamb. I hadn't heard him coming, so I was sure Ava hadn't either.

"I'm tired of him trying to boss me around anyways," Ava continued. "Crybaby." She sucked her teeth.

"Ava—" Chance tried to cut in.

"No Chance, I don't care. Just make my drink and I'll deal with Roman's mad ass later, yo." She huffed.

"Let me holler at you, love."

The surprised look on Ava's face made all of us burst into a fit of laughter.

"Ro—"

"Nah..." Roman spun around. "Come talk to me."

Ava smacked her lips and followed after her man.

"Y'all better not fuck in my bathroom either!" I called out and laughed when Chance gave me a knowing look.

Skyy began taking liquor and mixers out of the bags. "Ava is funny as hell." She shook her head.

"You ain't even seen the half of it." I chuckled reaching for my Beats pill. "Her ass should've been a comedian."

"Right," Chance cosigned.

After connecting my Bluetooth to the speaker, I searched through my playlists. "What y'all trying to hear?"

"Play Daniel Caesar's new album." Chance opened cabinets, getting everything she needed.

I nodded. After selecting his album and pressing on the first track, I headed back to the front of my home. I made it to the front door the same time Santonio entered carrying a box. I'd been with him all morning. He was deadset on me moving to the compound ASAP. I was only able to pack clothes.

I figured I'd start to furnish the place at the beginning of next week. So far, all the house had was a king bed in the master bedroom and groceries. I wasn't sure how I was going to fill up all the space. This house was a major upgrade from my house. I would probably end up hiring an interior decorator.

"Where you want this?" He sat the box down and stared at me. His hazel eyes seemed dimmer than usual. I knew it was because Deidra's funeral was in less than twenty-four hours. No one had really spoken on it. I guess we were all dealing with it in our own ways.

"You can leave it there." I eyed him. "You okay?"

He nodded. "Yeah, why you ask?"

I wanted to pull Santonio into a hug and kiss away his pain. "You want a drink?" I stepped closer to him.

He shook his head. "Nah, I'm bout to head to Ma Dukes then turn a couple corners."

I stared at him. "You coming back here tonight?"

Santonio ran his hand across his waves. "Nah."

"You're coming back to the compound though, right?"

"Probably."

*Probably.*

"If you don't come back here, where are you going?" Santonio had me fucked up.

"E, don't start that." He sighed.

I glared at him before I spun around and headed back to the kitchen.

"Come here, Erin."

I stopped in my tracks and faced him.

"I'm not going to lay up wit' no bitch."

"Okay." I didn't believe him.

"I just need to space to think about some shit." His eyes danced around me. "Don't take it personal, baby." He took a few strides and was right in front of me.

"I'm just trying to be here for you." I crossed my arms in defeat. I wasn't expecting Tone to cry on my shoulder, but if he wanted to talk, I was all ears.

"Don't worry about me, a'ight?" He rubbed his thumb gently across my jaw. "I love you."

"I know." I closed my eyes when he kissed my forehead.

THE RIDE TO THE CHURCH, besides Mozzy playing lowly, was silent. Even though Santonio paid for the family to ride in limos driven by his men, he insisted on driving his G-Wagon. I, of course, opted to ride with him. Sanaa and Toni were both in the backseat sleep. The weather sadly matched the day and our moods.

No sun. Just cloudy and grey skies. It was even sprinkling a little. I took Santonio's hand into mine and gave it slight squeeze. He had a stressed look on his face, and his eyes were bloodshot red.

"You good?" I asked, raising his arm and placing a soft a kiss on the back of his hand.

He nodded.

I then turned around to check on Sanaa and Toni. Toni was now awake looking out of her window and Sanaa was still knocked out. I smiled silently, thanking God for Santonio because without him, there would be no them. I faced forward and relaxed in my seat. My eyes rolled over to Santonio when he returned the kiss to the back of my hand.

# 6

## LIFE IS HARD...

### TONE

I sat on Ma Duke's porch, head low, in my feelings. The house was full of muthafuckas in mourning which was why I hadn't been inside yet. I didn't care that it was twenty degrees outside. I wanted to be by myself. I had too much on my mental to deal with other people.

The front door opened and closed, and then I waited for whoever it was that stepped out to pass by me. When her scent hit my nostrils, I looked over my shoulder. "What's wrong?"

Erin took a seat next to me. "Nothing." She unfolded the throw blanket in her hands.

"Where Sanaa and Toni?"

"Sleep." Erin scooted closer to me and wrapped the thick wool blanket around our shoulders. "You gon' get sick sitting out here." She rested her head on my arm.

"I ain't trippin." I had more important shit on my mind than catching a cold.

"I put you a plate up."

I nodded. I wasn't hungry neither.

We sat silent for a minute, and then E wrapped her right arm around my torso. "Remember when I had Sanaa and Deidra came to the hospital with a thousand bears?"

I chuckled. Erin was overexaggerating, but DeDe did show up with a bunch of teddy bears. Balloons too. She and Erin didn't really fuck with each other when they first met, but Deidra was at the hospital all day every day when Erin had Sanaa.

"She really loved and looked up to you." I could fell E staring at the side of my face. "I know you blame me, but..."

I looked over at her. "I don't blame you."

Our eyes stayed trained on each other.

"If I hadn't have gone out—"

"E..."

She looked off.

"DeDe got caught slippin'. Did she die over some petty bullshit? Yea. But ain't shit yo fault." I stared at her. "A'ight?"

Erin nodded.

I hung my head again and she kissed the side of my face.

"I wish I could take this hurt from you," she said sincerely.

"You being here is good enough."

We sat on the porch, in the cold, for a while before I told Erin to go in the house and warm up. She hesitated at first, but eventually she went in the house huffing and puffing with an attitude. I didn't need her sick. I cared about her health and well-being. Plus, if she got sick, Sanaa and Toni probably would too.

My phone ringing pulled me from my thoughts. I reached into my pocket for it and seen it was Xenia Masseria. She was Frank Masseria's only daughter and one of the richest women in the cartel. I was currently going through an expansion and Xenia was technically my partner.

"Wassup," I answered.

"Santonio..." Her soft voice seeped through the speakers. "Is this a bad time?"

"As a matter of fact, it is."

"Oh, okay. I won't take up too much of your time then. My father and Don Capporelli requested we meet soon to discuss business."

I closed my eyes.

"I was thinking we could meet in person."

"Xenia, I got some shit I need to take care of."

"I have a gift for you," she purred. "You won't want to miss this meeting, Santonio."

"Santonio."

Hearing Erin's voice made me look at the door. "Yeah, baby?"

"Come in. It's cold out here." She crossed her arms over her chest.

"Here I come," I assured her. Erin rolled her eyes and went back inside.

"So, I'll be seeing you soon?" Xenia pressed. "My father and Don Capporelli insist we get together sooner than later." She paused. "I do too."

I wasn't even in my suite good before my phone started ringing. Reaching into my pocket, I grabbed my phone and answered.

"Wassup?"

"Santonio," Xenia purred. "Have you landed?"

"I told you I would call you once I got settled." I massaged the bridge of my nose. "So, why are you calling?"

She chuckled. "You don't sound too pleased to hear from me."

I shook my head, already seeing the problems Xenia was about to come with.

"Please meet me in the hotel lobby in thirty minutes."

I hung up the phone and tossed it onto the bed next to me. I hadn't known Xenia for long but based off our short conversations here and there, she was bossy than a muthafucka. Short tempered too. The night of the Capporelli ball, she jumped over the bar and beat the bartender's ass for flirting with her date. Members of the Masseria family came and hauled her away just as she went to her thigh for her banger.

Xenia Masseria was trouble. But I had bigger issues at hand. Like taking care of this so I could find Bruce. Hakim said he was in Tivoli, so I was leaving in the morning. Roman, Que, Drake, and True were here and they were coming too.

After fixing the chains around my neck, I stood up. I was heading to the bathroom when there was a knock on the door. I frowned, pulling my piece from my side. I got to the door and looked through the peephole. I slipped my gun behind my back, still frowning. Pulling the door open, I stared back at Erin. I then stepped to the left to let her enter.

"What you doin' here, E?" I closed the door.

"Ava said y'all are leaving the country tomorrow..." She dropped a Louie V duffel bag and matching backpack on the bed. "So, she wanted to come and surprise Roman." Erin took a seat on the bed. "She's scared this might be the last time she will see him, so she has something special planned."

I eyed her, and she shrugged.

"She didn't wanna take the trip alone, so Me, Chance, and Skyy came."

"Where's Sanaa and Toni?'

"With your mom."

"You should be at home with them." I ran my palm across the top of my head. I had to tighten up on security after Deidra's death. I got too comfortable, had been too lenient, knowing nobody in Kansas City was stupid enough to fuck with me and mine.

"Ross and Royal are here."

I nodded.

"So, what you got planned for the night?" She surveyed me slowly.

"I got a business meeting in fifteen minutes."

"And after that?"

"I was gon' lay up, call you, and cake," I joked, and Erin chuckled. "But you here, so I'ma be in that all night."

Erin smirked, shaking her head.

"You hungry?"

"No. We ate on the jet."

I nodded just as my phone started ringing. Xenia's name flashed across the screen. "I should be back in a hour or two." I slipped my phone into my back pocket.

"Okay."

I made my way over to Erin and hovered over her. "Gimme a kiss..."

Our lips connected, and she closed her eyes. Sucking her bottom lip into my mouth, I gently bit down on it, tugged softly, and then let go. Erin opened her eyes and gazed up at me.

"I love you." I kissed her forehead. I knew her coming here was her way of being close to me just in case I didn't make it back home. We weren't in a relationship and despite all the bickering, she cared a lot about me. It didn't matter how hard E was, she was a woman first. A woman in love.

"I know."

~

"You look handsome."

I ignored Xenia and took a seat across from her.

"Would you like something to drink?"

"Nah."

"You sure?"

I nodded.

"My father and Don Capporelli speak very highly of you."

"Oh yeah?"

"Yes." She purred seductively. "You can do no wrong it seems." Xenia licked her lips.

Xenia was a certified bad bitch. Pretty brown eyes with full lashes and perfectly arched eyebrows. Her lips were plump and shiny, full like that Angelina Jolie chick. Her hair was black and silky, draping down her back and shoulders. She was model height, and her body was runway ready.

She was decked out in diamonds, sporting a tight black dress, exposing her smooth, golden skin. I licked my lips eyeing her fine ass.

Under different circumstances, I would've smashed Xenia. But I couldn't for two reasons: I didn't mix business with sex, and shit with me and E was going good. If I made it back from Tivoli in one piece, my family would be priority. I had plans for Erin Kincaid.

"Did you come alone?" Xenia looked around the restaurant and then towards the bar.

When I got down to the lobby, she changed her mind about leaving. Some shit about her feeling lightheaded because she hadn't eaten. I prayed Erin stayed in the room. Technically, I wasn't doing nothing wrong. I was taking care of business. E wouldn't see it like that, though.

"Nah, I came with family."

She nodded. "Are those your real eyes?"

I chuckled. "Yeah, they are. Are those your real titties?"

Xenia grinned. "Wanna find out?"

Tugging on my beard, I checked her out. "Why did you ask me to come here, Xenia?"

"Straight to the point, eh?" Her Italian accent was sexy. "I can get you Bruce."

I frowned.

"I've heard about the inconvenience he's caused the Capporelli family. My father contacted Don immediately, afraid that maybe the Capporellis weren't a good fit for the Masserias. He told Don he refused to do business with a divided family."

I continued pulling at my beard.

"Bruce Capporelli is..." She took a dainty sip from her glass. "A liability."

"Xenia, what type of games are you playing, shorty?"

"No games. Bruce thinks I've asked him here to conduct a side deal between him and the Masseria family." Xenia smiled. "Oh...and hopes of getting some pussy."

I glanced around the restaurant.

"I told Don Capporelli about Bruce's enthusiasm to steal from him. His own flesh and blood. Greedy...a snake."

"Can I get you anything to drink?" The waiter approached the table.

"Y'all got Ace?"

He nodded. "Yes. Dry?"

"Yeah."

He nodded before walking away.

"Why are you doing this, Xenia?"

"Because I see a God in you, Santonio."

I licked my lips.

"With you by my side, the Cartel could be *ours*." She took another sip. "Don Capporelli trusts you, men fear you, and my father respects you." Xenia chuckled. "And Papa is a hard man to please."

"No disrespect, Xenia, but I don't need you making plans for my future. Where is Bruce now?"

"He's meeting me in..." She looked down at the Cartier watch on her wrist. "Forty minutes."

"Where?"

The waiter sat my drink on the table and then refilled Xenia's champagne glass.

"He thinks we're meeting so he can pay me. He has his own driver and two other men with him. One Caucasian and one African American." Xenia bit down on the corner of her bottom lip. "Did those tattoos on your face hurt?"

I picked up my phone.

*Me: Change of plans*

"I figured the faster we take care of Bruce, the quicker we can work on us."

"*Us?*"

"Yes. I plan to be the Queen of the Candido Cartel. And you, my King."

I took a long drink from my glass.

"We could be untouchable."

My phone pinged.

*Ro: ?*

"Xenia, you fine, but I ain't even tryna get down like that, shorty." My eyes swept across the restaurant once more. When they landed on Chance, I silently prayed she was with True.

I guess God wasn't fuckin' wit' ya boy because Erin switched in right behind her.

# ERIN

Chance was saying something, but my focus was on Santonio. His hazel eyes stared right back at me. My gaze then shifted to the woman sitting at the table with him. She was talking but stopped when she noticed she didn't have his attention. When her eyes connected with mine, she frowned.

I returned the look.

*The fuck?*

I switched right to their table and looked down at Tone. "What is this?"

"Excuse you?"

I ignored her, eyes stayed trained on Santonio Keith Morris. My everything and my biggest headache.

"E, this is Xenia." His eyes dimmed, warning me to back down.

"This is business?" I'd only glanced at the Xenia chick briefly, but I couldn't deny her beauty. Sex appeal seeped through her pores.

"Yeah," he stated slowly.

"Santonio..."

I grimaced. No woman called him that besides me and Sadee. It didn't help that Xenia's accent made her sound like she was moaning.

"Who is your friend, *Dio*?" She smugly looked me up and down.

"E, go back to the room," Santonio dismissed me.

"Santonio," Xenia cooed. "We should be leaving." She pushed away from the table, her breasts practically spilling out of her dress. "I don't want to be late."

I stared back down at Tone.

"E..." he sighed.

I chuckled condescendingly. "You got it." I stepped away from the table and turned around. I made it to Chance who had a confused expression etched across her face.

"Who is she?"

I took a seat at the bar. "Business."

"Why are you so quiet?" Ava sat cross-legged on the carpet.

Chance, who was sitting in chair with her feet propped up on the end table, cleared her throat. "She's mad at Tone."

I smacked my lips. "No, I'm not. I just got a lot on my mind."

"Tone was downstairs at the restaurant with some woman. Then they left," Motor Mouth Chance said while polishing her toes.

Ava looked up from her phone. "He *what*?" She frowned.

"Her name was Xenia, and he said it was business."

A part of me...a *huge* part, felt like it was something more. The way Xenia cooed his name, looked at him. She gave off possessive vibes. And from my experience, women were only possessive when they were territorial. She'd called him *Dio*, which was *God* in Italian. When Santonio told me he spoke the language fluently, I'd begged him to teach me the basics. I went from learning simple words to speaking full sentences.

"Xenia Masseria." Ava sat her phone down next to her. "She's to the Masseria family what Tone is to the Capporellis. Important. A straight tycoon."

I nodded.

"I'm not supposed to be telling you this." She looked around. "Y'all gotta swear not to say anything."

My eyes rolled over to the left side of the suite's living room. "Chance..."

She zipped her lips playfully.

"Tone and Xenia are going through an expansion. They'll be working very closely from now on. Tone's the only person Don Capporelli trusts with that kind of power. Plus, his reputation is on the line and he knows Tone is solid."

"I can't believe I know people actually affiliated with the mob." Chance shook her head. "We're not safe. Our families aren't safe."

"Yes, we are. What happened to Deidra was done out of spite." Ava stood up. "Women *and* men fear Tone. He's like the Grim Reaper. No man is stupid enough to cross him."

"Bruce did," Chance stated sadly.

"Which is why Bruce is a dead man walking. Bruce only had the balls to come for Tone because of his last name. He's got Capporelli blood flowing through his veins."

I nodded. "So, Bruce has always had it out for Santonio?"

Ava shrugged. "From what I've seen, yeah. He's jealous. He ain't half the man Tone is, and the Don doesn't even try to hide his favoritism."

The room fell silent.

"Something must be up, though." Ava spoke. "Roman said they're not going to Tivoli."

Chance jumped up from her seat. "Swear?" The look of relief on her face didn't go unnoticed.

Ava's head bounced up and down. "Yep. That's the only reason I'm sitting here with y'all and not getting dicked down." She cheesed.

I smiled at her. Ava and Roman were perfect for one another. He allowed her to be herself, and in return, she gave him unwavering loyalty.

"Thank God..." Chance grabbed her phone.

"Where's Skyy?" Ava asked.

"With Que," Chance answered. "True said Que had something he wanted to do for her."

I knew Que was trying to help her out of her funk. The entire flight to Arizona, she stayed to herself. The reality of never seeing the guys again made us all emotional, but I knew Skyy's hurt doubled ours.

"We should hit up the spa tomorrow," Ava suggested, never one to miss out on an opportunity to pamper herself.

"Cool..." Chance carefully slipped her feet into her holographic PINK slides, and then faced me. "E, you down?"

I nodded, lifting my body from the couch. "Yeah."

"Bet." Ava grinned excitedly. "It's midnight now. Let's meet down at the lobby at eleven."

"Okay." I walked them to the door, opened it, and stepped to the side.

Chance made her exit first. "See you later, E."

"Later, Chance."

Ava followed, but then stopped and faced me. "E, don't sweat Xenia's thirsty ass. You, me, *and* Tone all know that bitch ain't got shit on you."

# 7

# IT DON'T HURT TO TRY

## TONE

"Who was that woman?" Xenia ran her hand up my arm.

"Why?"

"She didn't look too happy..." She chuckled. "You must be fuckin' her—"

I frowned. "Watch your mouth, Xenia." I wasn't about to explain who Erin was to me, but I wasn't about to allow Xenia to disrespect either. I learned a long time ago in the game, never show your weaknesses. Erin was and would always be my soft spot.

"So, I've hit a nerve?" Xenia smirked. "She's pretty. A little rough around the edges, but I can see why you love her."

I stared at her.

She looked out the window. "She'll be a problem."

"Xenia, shorty, don't mess this up," I said sternly. "Ain't shit between us gon' ever hit on a personal level." I opened the text conversation between me and E.

*Me: I love you*

Xenia's driver pulled the car into an unfinished, messy, dark construction site. There was another vehicle parked near a Port-a-Potty.

*Wifey: I know*

"Bruce is already here." Xenia took one last sip of the brown liquor in her glass and sat it down. "This should be interesting, Dio."

I stared at her.

"Stay here, my driver will give you the signal."

I sat my piece on my lap. "Hurry up."

I watched intently as Xenia made her way over to the Maybach Bruce was in. I stroked my beard when he stepped out and pulled her into a hug. Xenia said something that made him grin and laugh. When I noticed Bruce's driver open his door, I opened mine.

Xenia's pale faced chauffeur turned around to look at me. "Mr. Morris, Ms. Masseria insisted you stay inside."

"Fuck you." I hopped out. Wasn't no nigga or no bitch about to tell me what the fuck to do. I was my own boss. If I had to kill Xenia and her crew too, I would.

I pulled the trigger, and thanks to my silencer, Bruce's driver went down without his men knowing which way the shot came from. The other two gunmen who were with Bruce hopped out if the car simultaneously. Xenia's driver got out the car and hit one, sending him crumbling. My second shot sent his last man down. Xenia pressed her burner against Bruce's temple with a smile on her face as I approached them, gun still pointed. Bruce's gaze landed on me and the fear in his eyes made my dick hard.

"T-Tone..." he stuttered.

"Wassup, Bruce." I smirked.

He looked to Xenia. "You fuckin' whore! You stupid, mixed breed bitch!"

Xenia hit Bruce hard over the head and he fell. "Tahil..." She addressed her driver. "Put him in the trunk."

I GOT BACK to the hotel an hour and a half later.

"Santonio...I'll see you tomorrow, no?"

I eyed Xenia as my tongue swiped quickly across my bottom lip.

"We will do great things together."

I chuckled as I opened my door. "Yo, Xenia—"

"Santonio, I usually get my way."

Getting out of her car, I shut the door and made my way towards the entrance. When I stepped into the lobby, Roman, Que, Drake, True, and Ross were waiting for me.

"Where that nigga at?"

I motioned for them to follow me back towards the entrance. "Ross, bring the truck around."

He nodded and then walked off.

"How you know you can trust this Xenia bitch?" Roman crossed his arms. "What if she a snake?"

"Xenia ain't a snake." I stroked my beard. "She got a agenda, though."

"Which is?" Que finally spoke.

"Let me handle Xenia." I checked the time on my Patek Phillip. Seeing it was almost two in the morning, I knew E was going to have an attitude. But I had shit to take care of.

AFTER PLUGGING in the location where Xenia had Bruce dropped off, we arrived damn near in the middle of nowhere. Ross parked a few feet away from a black Chevy Impala and we all exited the truck. We stood at the trunk and, just as I was about to speak, Drake sprayed the entire back of the whip with bullets. Once he emptied the clip, I counted back from five and looked at him.

"Chill." I didn't want Bruce's death to be quick. He had to suffer.

Drake sucked his teeth. "Fuck that...you seen what that nigga did to DeDe?"

Taking the key Xenia gave me out of my pocket, I popped the trunk. Bruce laid balled up, whimpering. He had a bullet in his arm, one in his leg and another in his chest. True snatched him out and dropped him on the ground.

"Shut yo bitch ass up!" Roman barked.

Bruce cried harder.

"Bruce Capporelli..." I started. "You done fucked up, bruh."

Que chuckled.

"Santonio." Bruce groaned. "You don't wanna do this." He coughed. "My father..."

I grabbed him up by his collar.

"I'll pay you," he wheezed. "I'll...give you whatever you want." The nigga started crying. "Don't do this."

I stole on him, sending blood spewing from his nose and his head flying backwards.

"I—"

My fist crashed into his face again...then again...then again, and again.

"Let me in on that." Roman's foot came down hard on Bruce's head. He then stomped him repeatedly until Que pulled him back.

Bruce's cries grew louder.

"Crybaby ass nigga, let me finish this nigga, Tone." Drake went to his side for his burner.

"Nah..." I stared down at Bruce. "True, hand me that hatchet."

True went back to the trunk.

"Santonio," Bruce whispered. "Xenia can't be tru—"

Roman kicked him.

I took the hatchet from True. "You killed our sister." I knelt down. "Because of what?" I asked through a clenched jaw. "Jealousy?"

He'd damaged my family. If Erin was my right hand then DeDe had been my left. My little sister...she didn't deserve to die like that.

"Grab his left arm," I instructed.

True yanked Bruce's arm. Bringing the hatchet down, I disconnected his hand from his body. Bruce's agonizing screams pierced through the night. With snot and tears rolling down his face, he called out for God. He begged for me to please have mercy on him.

Mercy?

Nah, fuck that.

Where was Deidra's mercy? When she cried out for help, where was her pity?

"Drake, grab that gas can."

When he retrieved it, he immediately doused Bruce's bloody, limp body until the container was empty. When he was finished, I stared down at Bruce. He was crying and screaming, but we all stood in a circle around him unmoved. Taking the matches out of my pocket, I set it on fire and tossed the flame onto Bruce. A blaze of fire instantly engulfed him. As the smell of burning flesh filled my nostrils, I smirked, momentarily satisfied.

Ro, Que, True, and Drake pulled out their burners and emptied their clips into his burning body. I took the blunt from behind my ear, sparked it up and put it to my lips. I took a couple hits and passed the L to Roman. We stood silently, passing the weed as we watched Bruce's body burn to a crisp. Even though we'd avenged Deidra's death, my heart felt numb. A nigga felt empty.

# ERIN

When my phone went off the next morning, a tired groan escaped from my lips. I rolled over only to bump into Santonio. He pulled me close and then shifted in his sleep a little.

"Who calling you this early?" he mumbled.

"I don't know."

"Better not be no nigga."

I chuckled, and my phone went off again.

Reluctantly, Santonio let me go.

I turned sideways and reached for my phone on the dresser. Santonio wrapped his big arms around my waist and kissed my neck. Seeing Sadee's name flash across the screen made an instant smile grace my face because I already knew who was on the other end.

"Hello." I shuddered involuntarily when Santonio licked and nibbled on my earlobe.

"Hi Mommy." Sanaa's tiny, squeaky voice warmed my heart.

I put her on speaker. "Hi, Naa-Naa."

"Mommy..." I knew she was pouting. "Where are you?"

"I'm with Daddy." I closed my eyes, enjoying the feel of Santonio's hand gently exploring my body.

"Hi Daddy," Sanaa said excitedly.

"Sup, Naa-Naa." He stopped caressing me.

"Say hi, Toni," Sanaa said, making Tone and I chuckle.

"Toni-noni..." Tone's raspy voice was funny when he was in daddy mode.

Toni's babbling made me smile harder.

"I love you too, Toni-noni..."

She babbled some more.

"I love you, Daddy," Sanaa jumped in.

"I love you more," he told her, hugging my body.

"Mommy?"

"I love you *and* Toni." I sunk into Tone's chest. "Give her kisses for me."

"Kay..." Sanaa said and then we heard her give little kisses to her baby sister. "Mommy, Granny said we gotta eat."

"Okay, Naa. Call Mommy when you get done." I sighed.

"Bye, Mommy."

After I ended the call, Santonio wasted no time pushing my panties to the side. I poked my butt out to give him further access and he rubbed the head of his dick along my kitty.

"I love you, E," he whispered with his lips on my earlobe.

I bit down on my bottom lip. "I know."

"I ain't ever gon' stop fighting for my family." Santonio's doughy lips connected with my neck. "You gotta fight wit' me, though. I know you got your guard up baby..." He planted a wet kiss on me. "And I ain't gon even front like you shouldn't."

I trembled when he dipped his dick in me and he pulled back out.

"I need you by my side, E." Santonio fucked me slowly with the tip of his dick.

I widened the gap between my legs.

"I'ma wife you one day," he promised. "Sooner than later."

"Mmm..." I fucked him back slowly, wanting to feel all of him. When he pulled at the way out, I frowned. "Santonio..."

"What?"

I smacked my lips and tried to get out of bed.

He chuckled, yanking me back into his chest. "What you got a attitude for?"

"Because you play too much." My pussy was dripping, mind set on the nut I knew Santonio could give me.

"Lil' freaky ass." He slapped me hard on the side of my ass and it jiggled.

"I gotta get dressed." I found myself pouting. "I'm meeting the ladies at twelve."

"What you got that bottom lip poked out for?" He called me out. The amusement in his tone made me try to pull away from him again to no avail.

"It's like that?" Santonio put a hickey on my neck.

"Stop putting hater marks on me." Even though I was talking shit, I loved the way he sucked on my neck. His lips were so soft and full.

"Shut up," he mumbled. "And take these muthafuckas off." Santonio tugged at my underwear. "This too." He removed my shirt roughly.

"Ouch!" I hit him on the arm. "You almost snatched my nose ring out." I massaged the hoop in my nose.

"Quit crying and get yo spoiled ass on top." He laid on his back and pulled his dick from the top of his Versace briefs. "I want a boy."

I rolled my eyes. "Is that how you talk to me? 'Get on top'?" I mocked him. "So much for foreplay." I blinked, and he was on his knees pulling me by my waist to the middle of the bed.

"You hard-headed." He slid my panties off. Santonio stared down at me lustfully and I blushed. I actually looked away and bit the inside of my cheek to keep from smiling.

He squeezed my thighs and chuckled lightly. "You want some foreplay, baby?" he said all sexy and my love throbbed.

I stared right back at him lustfully...in love.

"Cause this pussy is already soaked." He leaned forward, lifted my thighs and pushed them back. Santonio then commenced to placing kisses on my clit. "I got you, though." He blew lightly, and my body reacted with a slight tremor.

I grabbed the back of his head and pushed my pussy further into his face. "Santonio..." I whined when his tongue flickered quickly against my nub and then he stopped.

"Shut up." His raspy voice was laced with yearning.

For the first time in a long time, Santonio didn't have to tell me to do something twice. His tongue dipped into my opening and then slithered up my pussy. He latched onto my clit and zoned in on it.

"Sshhhit." My hips rocked back and forth.

He let my legs go and I held them up on my own. Santonio's middle finger entered me and he finger fucked me with the 'come here' motion. I looked down at him as he put in work, turned the fuck on. The tattoos, his body, the waves spinning in his head, and them damn hazel eyes when he looked back at me had me cumming prematurely. And hard as hell.

My body bucked widely as I released, and he licked up every drop. With my eyes barely open, I watched him run his hand down his mouth and then come completely out of his briefs. I lifted my body up slowly when he laid next to me on his back and stroked his manhood. Squatting into the reverse cowgirl position, I slowly slid down on the dick. I'd forgotten how much of a perfect fit Santonio was.

You ever had dick so good, you get those 'ASMR' tingles? Yeah ...that's what dick from Santonio did. I could feel the tingles from the top of my head to tip of my toes. They amplified when I started bouncing and rode the dick like a champ. Santonio gripped my waist tightly and a low moan escaped from him.

*Guess I got that 'ASMR' pussy.*

I smirked.

"Fuck...E." He tried to hold me still.

I stood on my tippy toes, put my hands on my knees and made my ass clap, making sure he hit the back of my pussy every time.

"This my dick?" I looked back.

He moaned, making the sexiest love face.

The sight had me moaning too. I rose up just enough to only ride the tip of his dick and picked up the pace, driving his ass wild.

"I love you, E." He slapped both of my ass cheeks at once. "This yo dick."

"I know..." I could feel my second orgasm building, so I dropped all the way down.

Tone used that as leverage, gripped my hips tight, and pounded me.

"You gon stop fighting me?" He went harder.

I held onto his hands. "Yes!"

"You gon' come back home?"

"Yes, baby!" My eyes rolled to the back of my head.

"You gon' give Daddy a boy?"

"Yes!" The way Santonio's dick had me seeing stars, in that moment I was ready and willing to give him twenty boys if he wanted. "I'm cumming!"

"Shit..." He panted. "Me too, baby."

We came together, me screaming how much I loved him and him jerking hard, holding me tight.

8

# MY BROTHER'S KEEPER... SISTER'S PROTECTOR

ERIN

I was an hour late meeting up with the ladies thanks to Santonio's healthy sexual appetite. He wouldn't let me take a shower, get dressed or do my hair in peace. It got to a point where I caught a full-blown attitude because my kitty was sore and swollen. He finally let me go when I snapped on his ass and told him to leave me alone. He laughed at me and called me a crybaby, but eventually let me go.

"Bout time." Ava wasted no time going in on me. "Limping and shit."

Chance giggled.

I rolled my eyes. "Whatever."

"Don't feel bad." Chance draped her arm over my shoulders. "Skyy isn't coming and Ava *just* got down here." She gave Ava the side eye.

Ava shrugged.

"What's wrong with Skyy?" We made our way towards the exit.

"She said she's not in the mood." Chance slipped her sunglasses on. "True told me Que is going to spend the day with her."

I nodded.

"Let's do brunch first," Ava suggested, texting on her phone. "My sisters are here." She beamed. "Is it cool if we meet up wit' em?"

"I don't mind." Chance looked to me for approval.

I usually didn't clique up with chicks I didn't know, but if Ava claimed they were good people, then I trusted her judgment.

"I'm down."

THIRTY MINUTES LATER, we ended up at "Teaspoon." We'd only just arrived, but Ava had already managed to snap on the hostess *and* the waiter. I only shook my head; you couldn't take her ass nowhere. It was only one, but she was live and on one. Chance had to make her promise to behave when we were finally seated and our orders were placed.

"I'm finna smash this shit. All that fuckin done made me work up a serious appetite, yo."

"I still don't see how you're not pregnant yet." Chance took a drink of water.

Ava frowned. "Birth control." She turned her nose up. "I can't afford to be popping out babies right now." She shook her head disapprovingly. "What Nicki say? 'Ain't pushing out his babies til he buy the rock.'"

I chuckled.

"Anyway, between Kiddo, my nieces and nephews, True's trouble-makers, and the ladybugs, I don't need a kid. I'll just share them."

Chance laughed. "Don't do my babies."

"Chase and Chasity *are* bad." I had to agree with Ava.

"That's because their mamas let them do whatever they want." Chance frowned. "True had to pop Chassy pooh for saying she had a 'phatty.'"

Ava's silly ass burst into a fit of laughter. "True gon' have fun wit' that one."

I shook my head.

"Ladies..." The waiter sat down glasses of red wine in front of us.

"Will the rest of your party be joining you soon?"

"As a matter of fact..." Ava's eyes shot towards the entrance and her voice trailed off. A wide smile spread across her face, she pushed her chair back, and stood up. "B! Over here!"

Patrons in the restaurant eyed our table. My gaze landed on the front of the packed restaurant to see four women walking in our direction. They were all gorgeous, all dressed to kill, smiling as they made their way to the table. Chance and I played the background as Ava approached them and they took turns giving her loving embraces.

"When did y'all get here?" Ava led them back to us.

The chick who resembled Lisa-Raye in her prime rubbed the small pudge on her belly. "This morning."

Ava nodded. "Kai said the guys were coming, he didn't mention y'all." Seeing Ava so happy and bubbly made me smile a little. You could feel the love between the group.

Once they made it to the table, Ava introduced them. "Blaze, Ryan, Jaime, and Kenya..." She looked down. "These are my home-girls Erin and Chance." Ava pointed. "They family too."

Everyone said "hey" simultaneously.

"It's nice to finally meet y'all." The chick she pointed out as Jaime smiled.

"Right," Kenya co-signed. "We've heard a lot about y'all."

"All good I hope." I smiled, already knowing Ava wasn't the type to talk bad about you behind your back and then smile in your face. She'd gladly tell you exactly what she was thinking and how she felt with no fucks given.

Chance stood. "I give hugs." She giggled. "Any family of Av's is family of mine."

Blaze grinned. "My kind of girl." She and Chance shared a quick hug.

One by one, she embraced each woman, complimenting either their hair, nails, or beauty. Chance got to Ryan, who had a look of discomfort on her face.

"I don't bite," Chance joked, causing everybody to laugh.

Ryan reluctantly fell into Chance's hug, chuckling.

Once everyone was seated, the waiter took their orders and promised to be right back with their drinks.

"So..." Kenya removed her jacket. "Av, what's new?"

"Girl, nothing. I see you bustin' out your clothes again. You and Cole workin' on a football team?"

We all laughed when Kenya flipped her the bird.

"Don't be hatin'." She snickered.

"You know what you having?" Chance asked.

"Another boy and I already have two." Kenya pouted. "Y'all, I swear, after this I'm getting my tubes tied, clipped and burnt."

I chuckled. "I got two girls, so I know how you feel."

"Let's swap one."

The table filled with laughter again.

"I have my boy and girl, so I'm done." Blaze beamed proudly. "No more for me."

"I second that," Ryan cosigned. "Raine is all I can handle."

Jaime snickered. "Which is why we switch off. Duke's little ass drives me crazy, yo."

Chance cheesed. "We were just trying to see what Ava was waiting on." She put Av on blast.

Ava downed her drink. "Quit tryna auction off my uterus."

Again...laughter, snickers, and giggles erupted from every lady at the table. That was pretty much how the rest of brunch went. Ava and Kenya saying something hilarious, drinks flowing, good conversation, and even greater food. Kenya begged us not to tell Cole she'd had a glass of wine, and even though Blaze was against it, she promised. Even after we ate and the waiter cleared the table, for over an hour we sat around talking and getting to know each other.

When we finally did part ways, we exchanged numbers, and promised to link up that night. Ava and Chance rolled out with the ladies, and I called Skyy. I knew Chance said she was spending the day with Que, but me and my sister needed some quality time. Skyy must've been feeling the same way because she happily obliged to meet me at the, "Mini Time Machine."

~

"E...WHERE DID YOU BRING ME?" Skyy stopped to look at the miniature piece on display.

I laughed. The museum was something I had googled last minute and thought would be interesting. "I wanted to try something new. Experience something different."

She smacked her lips. "You're so extra." Standing up straight, Skyy looked around the room. "So how was brunch? Your eyes are glossy as hell, so you must've had a good time."

Nodding, I texted Santonio back. "I did. Ava's people from New York are here. They're cool as hell."

"Ryan and Kenya are here?"

"Yeah...you know them?"

"Not for real. I met 'em once, back when me and Que were still fuckin' around."

"Mmm...'bout that. What's up with you and Mr. Que'Darius?"

Skyy rolled her eyes. "Nothin'. I don't know why he's trying to babysit my feelings all of a sudden."

"Because he cares about you, Skyy."

"Yeah, yeah." She waved me off. "So, you and Tone good?"

I shrugged. "To be honest, Skyy, I don't know what we're doing." Even though we'd had sex, and I confessed my love for him, there were still some things that hadn't been settled between us. "I feel like being with him goes against everything I've been saying and every point I've been trying to prove."

"This have anything to do with Nette?"

We walked in silence.

"E, I loved Nette just as much as you did, but quit actin' like she was this perfect fuckin' person. How many times did she say fuck you? Or go behind your back tellin' your business to a bitch that hated your guts? How many times did you have to come to her rescue? Or bail her out of *her* bullshit, cause of the choices *she* made?"

"Sky—"

"No, E...stop." She faced me. "How many times were you there when it mattered the most? For all of us?"

We stopped walking.

"Quit feeling guilty for loving Tone. Quit blaming yourself for Nette's death. And stop crying over spilled fuckin' milk. Cause at the end of the day, life goes on."

We took off again.

"I already told Sasha she was wrong."

I rolled my eyes. "Sasha is the very least of my concerns right now."

"Her ass is just going though it..."

"Ain't we all?"

"Ain't that the truth?" she said sadly.

"Skyy...I'm sorry about everything you're dealing with. I know Deidra held special place in your heart."

She shrugged. "I set myself up for disappointment, E. I couldn't have DeDe because of who her father is. And I can't have Que because technically I'm 'lovin' the crew.'"

I cringed at her choice of words. When Skyy met Que, she didn't know he knew Tone and his people.

"That's shit I gotta learn to live with. Ain't no use in feeling sorry for myself. Yeah, I'm sad DeDe is gone, and yes, I'm hurt that Que keeps toying with my emotions. But ain't no point in dwelling on it."

"You know if you wanna come back home, both you and Skylar have a room at my house."

She nodded. "I know."

A comfortable silence lingered between us as we journeyed through the museum, lost in our thoughts, trapped in our gloomy reality. I wanted happiness and a peace of mind for everybody I loved and cared about. It killed me knowing there was nothing I could do to ease Skyy's mind or give her the reassurance that life was going to get better. Blinking back tears, I hooked my arm into hers. In return, she gave me a slight squeeze.

# TONE

Jay-Z's, "Can't be life" played lowly from the suite's built in Bose speakers as I stared down at the weapons on the floor. Bruce was dead, but it wasn't enough. I would've rather went to war, battled, and died in a blaze of glory. I took a toke of the weed in the backwood I'd rolled not too long ago. Soon after, I took a long sip from the lean in a double Styrofoam cup.

A nigga was going through it. I felt like a failure. I was letting everybody in my life down—Erin, Ma Duke, my daughters...my Empire. I ran my free hand down my face and sighed. I needed to get some shit under control. Even if I had to end innocent lives...I didn't care.

In my line of business, being understanding wasn't tolerated. I'd been too chill lately. Gave niggas the opportunity to infiltrate my operation...break my family and my heart. Poor Deidra had been a casualty. The only wrong thing baby girl did was count on me to keep her safe.

I took another long gulp of the purple liquid in my cup and chuckled. Wasn't shit funny, but my Empire would definitely get the last laugh, even if I had to lay my life on the line. I was ready and willing, though. That was the life I chose, this was the shit I'd become accustomed to. Pain had been a normalcy my entire lifespan, the evils of the world were my foundation. I took that shit on the chin, though.

I finished off the weed, thinking about my next tat. For me, tattoos were nothing but bruises, and I had a body full. I was bruised and broken, but a nigga was blessed. I had a good woman in my corner, two beautiful baby girls, and an army full of soldiers that respected me. Life was all about wins and losses...that I accepted humbly.

Which was why I'd paid for every close member on my team to be here in Tucson. Hotels, rentals, food, and other expenses were all on me. I knew they could cover their own shit, but just like E and my lil mamas, they were a reflection of me. Losing Deidra, we'd taken a major loss. That was why I needed to be surrounded by love, and most importantly, loyalty. I knew that the moment Erin Kincaid entered my suite twenty-four hours ago.

Instead of mourning over DeDe's death, we needed to celebrate her life. Prove she hadn't died in vain. I missed my dawg. But one day, I'd see her again. Knowing DeDe, she'd probably be waiting on the other side, a blunt in hand, smiling hard. Anticipating my arrival.

## 9

# DOWN TO RIDE TIL THE VERY END

ERIN

"Y ou coming up to Ava's room for the pre-turn up, right?" Chance asked on the other end of the phone.

I stared at my reflection. After returning to the hotel, Skyy and I went our separate ways. Santonio was gone, and I'd taken a much-needed nap after all the sex and drinks I'd had earlier. Now it was almost midnight and I had a whole lot more energy. After talking to Sanaa when I woke up, Ava called and informed me everybody was going clubbing.

"Yes ma'am. Give me ten minutes." I adjusted the iced out different length chokers around my neck. "Let me call Skyy and tell her."

"No need to. Ryan already went to get her because she tried to change her mind about coming out."

I shook my head. "Okay, I'll be down there."

"Hurry, E."

"Kay." I hung up and tossed my phone onto the bed.

I stared right back at my reflection and combed through my hair. It was bone straight and parted down the middle. It looked silkier than usual, making it look like a weave, but it was all me. I'd kept my makeup subtle, only really focusing on my eyebrows, lashes and lipstick.

It was chilly out, but I decided on a long sleeve, grey dress with a deep v-cut that stopped right between my breasts. The silk material hugged my body tight, accentuating my curves, and stopped right at the middle of my thighs. The imprint from my nipple rings made it even sexier. And if that wasn't enough, the entire back was out. I paired the dress with clear, five-inch stilettos that probably looked like stripper heels, but I didn't give a fuck.

I usually kept my jewelry low-key, but tonight, I'd gone all out. I was iced the fuck out. My earrings, chokers, watch, bracelets and anklet were white diamonds that looked see through. Hell, even my nose ring was shining, and although you couldn't see my nipple rings, they'd cost a hefty penny. All gifts that Santonio had bought me any time he went to see his jeweler.

*Kash Doll would be proud if she saw me.*

I chuckled at that thought. I hadn't planned to wear all this ice at once, but I figured, why not. We weren't even supposed to still be in Arizona. Chance, Skyy, and I were supposed to be in Vegas on a mini vacay by now. We'd decided that once the men left, we needed a getaway from everything.

Satisfied with my wardrobe, I grabbed my diamond studded clutch. I slipped my phone in, made sure I had my ID and made my exit. As I made my way down the hall, I got eyes from a few men who were walking past me. One even tried to grab my attention with, "Hey Ma," but I ignored him. I stepped onto the elevator the same time my phone went off.

"That gotta be your man blowing you up."

I looked to my left to see a very handsome brotha in a navy blue, tailored suit, and shiny expensive dress shoes on his feet. His Caesar cut looked fresh, and he smelled good as hell.

Pressing on the button to take me down to Ava's floor, I ignored him too.

"I'm just saying, if my woman was out here looking this stunning, she'd be on my arm." He chuckled. "Not on an elevator alone with a nigga like me."

Still, I ignored him.

"Smelling all good and shit."

When I looked at him again, he licked his lips while eyeing me.

The elevator made a dinging sound and I pulled my gaze away from his. I checked to make sure I was on the right floor before stepping off.

"Take care of yourself, beautiful. Don't break too many hearts tonight."

I walked away, smiling, definitely feeling myself now. When I got near Ava's room, I could hear loud music. I opened my clutch to remove my phone the same time the door swung open and I came face to face with Ryan. Her makeup and curly blonde hair were flawless. A tight, black, off the shoulder dress clung to her body, exposing two arm full of colorful tattoos. Black thigh high boots completed her look.

"I was just about to come get yo ass." She laughed, making room for me to get by.

I chuckled, entering the room. Trina's, "Bad Bitch Anthem" was blasting loud as we made our way through the suite.

"Bout fuckin' time!" Ava approached, grinning. "Fine ass!"

I shook my head at her drunk ass. Ava was a chocolate beauty. The very definition of melanin magic. Her signature pixie cut was slayed to perfection as usual. In her red, strapless dress, and silver strappy stilettos, Ava could've been on the cover of any magazine. I then looked around the room at all the ladies and it looked like a music video set.

Jaime in her black long-sleeved dress and long, silky, curly ponytail, looked like a doll. Blaze in her white two piece, with a body to die for, was definitely killing shit. Even pregnant Kenya with her naked ass was a sight for sore eyes. Her black, spaghetti strap dressed didn't leave much for the imagination. But Chance...

*True is going to have a fit.*

Her beige, sheer, two-piece set was more revealing than a little bit.

It didn't help Chance was thick as hell. A slick, shiny bun sat on the top of her head, and the only jewelry she had on were the studs in her ears. Yeah, True was going to ruin everybody's night.

"My bitches bad, lookin like a bag of money!" Ava had her phone out, most likely on Snapchat.

We all laughed as I noticed Skyy wasn't in the room.

"Where's Skyy?"

Chance handed me a Ciroc bottle. "She said she doesn't feel good."

I sighed.

"Let her mourn in peace, E." Chance looked at me sadly.

"I told her we would kick it for her," Ryan assured me as Jaime handed me the blunt.

I nodded, taking a pull.

After finishing off three blunts, taking a few shots of Ciroc and posing for plenty of pictures, we left the suite on one. When we got to the lobby, Royal, my new driver, led us to a Black Cadillac Escalade stretch limo. Once we were all in securely, I removed my phone from my clutch and shot Skyy a text.

*Me: I love you. Call me if you need me or wanna talk.*

"She'll be okay." Blaze tapped my thigh. "Give her some space."

"This one is for DeDe!" Ava screamed, popping open a bottle of champagne.

# TONE

Erin entered the VIP, swagged the fuck out. The beat dropped, and Cardi B started spittin'. E bent over, stuck her ass out, and popped that phat muthafucka like a stripper bitch, with Ava and Kenya egging her on. I smirked. I didn't care that all eyes were on her. She belonged to me. And every nigga here knew that.

She stood up straight, still dancing, rapping along with song. Ryan slapped her on the butt, laughing, hyping her fine ass up even more. My baby mama was dope as fuck. I loved seeing her in her zone with no cares. She deserved to live like this every night. I took a drink out of the D'ussé bottle I had been babysitting.

She stopped dancing and started hyping Chance up. True pushed the bitch on his lap onto the floor and made his way over to them. I only shook my head.

"That nigga stay cock blockin' Channy." Roman chuckled. "Come here, Ava Lane!" he called out and she wasted to no time switching over to him.

"Hey baby." She dropped down in his lap and they shared a kiss.

The few bitches in our VIP who weren't permanently tied to nobody in my crew screwed their faces up at the exchange. I chuckled, tossing the bottle back again. Other than my guys from New York, and my family, I'd flown Gunz, Chris, Javier, and a few of their peoples out. We were taking up the entire section and the one right next to it.

My eyes landed back E, who was now chitchatting with Nas' chick.

"Who this bitch think she is?" I overheard a chick say.

"Right," her homegirl co-signed.

"Jewelry probably fake as fuck."

My gaze shifted over to a dope lil mami who had been trying to get my attention all night.

"Her ass too." They slapped fives, giggling.

My eyes rolled back over to Erin and I smirked. Obviously, these birds hadn't ever fucked with a boss ass nigga. Wasn't shit on Erin fake but her lashes. We made eye contact, and I threw my chin up letting her know to bring that ass here. Everybody made room for her to get by as she glided towards me.

When she was within arms reach, I stood up and pulled her into a hug.

"Damn, E. You fuckin' a nigga head up right now, baby," I whispered in her ear. I let her go, gently took her hand into mine, and spun her around slowly. "I see you, shorty."

She looked up at me lustfully. "Thank you."

"Nah..." I eyed her hungrily. "Thank you." I wrapped my arms around her waist. "We ain't gon' make it back to the room without me gettin' up in that."

She chuckled.

"So, don't even count on it." Erin would be lucky if we made it to the whip. "Lookin' like a open safe and shit."

She laughed. "You stupid."

"Gimme a kiss," I demanded. Shit, a nigga would've begged if she asked me to.

Erin's lips connected with mine, and I pulled her closer. Our tongues collided, and I could taste the mints she'd had. My free hand ran across her left ass cheek and I gave it a firm squeeze.

"Y'all gon' start fuckin' or what?"

Reluctantly, I pulled away from our kiss, and gently wiped the corner of Erin's mouth before running my hand down my own.

"Right." Roman co-signed True.

Me and E stared at each other for a moment before I gave True's hatin' ass my attention.

"Stay outta grown folks' business, youngin.'" I took a seat on the plush leather sectional and pulled Erin into my lap.

"True..." Chance whined. "I'm 'bout to go to the bar."

He mugged her. "No, the fuck you not. I don't even know why you put this shit on. Who you tryna look cute for?"

Chance rolled her eyes.

"It's bottles all through this muthafucka. Pick ya poison and find a seat."

The chicks from earlier laughed out loud and Chance's face flushed red from embarassment.

Erin's head snapped in their direction. "The fuck is so funny?"

"Exactly." Ava leaned forward. "You bitches got a problem?"

"Ava Lane..."

"Nah." True stared down at them. The amusement in his eyes had been replaced with dark threatening ones. "I wanna know the answer to both questions." He pulled Chance closer to him defensively. "You got somethin' you wanna say to my shorty?" He made the burner on his hip visible.

"True..." Chance stepped in front of him. "I have to use the bathroom." She grabbed both sides of his face when he wouldn't take his eyes off of them. "Walk with me, please."

True looked down at Chance and his face softened. "Come on." He took her hand into his and they walked away.

Ava laughed. "Chance can make that nigga do anything. You bitches 'a-kee-keeing' and she just saved your life."

"Ava Lane..."

"Bitches got spooked *real* quick." She laughed. "I would've let him put a bullet in ya head, yo. Mojo jojo lookin' ass bitches."

"Come talk to me." Roman tapped her leg lightly.

Ava's bottom lip dropped, but she got up and they took off towards the bathroom.

Erin laughed, taking the bottle out of my hand.

My eyes shifted to Beavis and Butthead. "Beat it."

They hopped up simultaneously and stormed out of the VIP. I paused momentarily when Xenia entered, followed by her security. Her eyes scanned the room quickly, and when they landed on me, she smirked. I fixed E in my lap and wrapped my arm around her tighter. I hoped Xenia wasn't on no bullshit.

"Dio..." She smiled. "I didn't know you'd be here."

Erin's body tensed.

"Sup, Xenia."

She looked around. "Oh, nothing much." She then pouted play-fully. "No invite for me? We had such a great night."

Erin placed the bottle in her hand on the ground.

"Did you want something?" I frowned. Xenia was tripping. The last thing I needed was for my baby to think we'd smashed.

Xenia looked down at Erin. "Nice to see you again. Erin, is it?" she stated smugly.

"Stop talkin' to me," E said coolly.

Xenia smiled. "I was only being cordial. No need to be hostile."

"Xenia..."

Her eyes shifted to me. "I'll call you later, Dio." She then turned around and switched back out of the VIP.

"You fucked her? And don't lie," Erin gritted with her back to me. "I swear to God, if I feel like you lying, I'ma smash this bottle over your head."

I sighed. "Nah...I ain't fucked her."

"You want to?"

"Nah."

"She wanna fuck you?"

"Yeah."

She nodded.

"E..."

"Santonio, I'm not giving out any more chances."

"I know, baby."

"I swear to God." Her voice cracked.

Squeezing her waist firmly, I kissed her exposed back. "I got you."

# 10

## MY LIFE IS A MESS

### ERIN

A fter three days in Arizona, I was back on Missouri soil. My first priority was getting to my ladybugs. I'd never gone this long without seeing them, and FaceTime didn't count. I needed to smell them, kiss on tiny cheeks, and give big hugs. They'd been staying with Sadee, but she had let my mom get them the last day.

When Royal pulled the black 2019 Rolls-Royce Cullinan Tone bought for him to drive me around in front of my mom's house, a huge smile spread across my face. He could barely put the vehicle in park before I grabbed the handle and let myself out. Thankfully, I was bundled up in a grey puffer coat with the Chanel hat, glove, and scarf to match because the cold weather was harsh as hell.

I climbed my mother's stairs feeling giddy just knowing I would be reunited with my favorite little ladies in just a few minutes. I rang the door bell, and then looked around.

"Who is it?" I heard Erica ask from the other side of the door.

"Erin." I waited for her to open the door. When she did, the attitude radiating off of her made me frown. "What's wrong?" I asked, stepping into the warmth of my mother's home.

"Your mama is irritating me, bro." She crossed her arms. "I'm coming to your house." She took off up the stairs, most likely going to her room to pack an overnight bag.

I ventured down the hall and to the living room where my mother was feeding Toni and watching television.

"Hi baby," I squealed, damn near running to my mini me. Her brown eyes landed on me and she cheesed. When I reached her, I picked her up and kissed her quickly on her small lips, not caring about the mashed potato mess on her face.

"Hello to you too, Erin." My mother sighed. "I thought you weren't coming back until tomorrow."

I hugged Toni tight. "I was, but I told Santonio I was missing my babies." I glanced around the room. "Where's Sanaa?"

"She's upstairs sleep."

I nodded. "Toni, did you miss Mommy?" I placed my forehead on hers, stared into her innocent eyes, and swayed side to side. "'Cause I missed you."

"Are you sure it's not because you knew Sadee dropped them off with me?" My mom stood and started cleaning up.

I looked at her, confused. "What? What are you talkin' about?"

"I mean, when Sadee had them, you weren't in a rush to get home. But as soon as they get over here, you wanna leave early and come home."

I frowned. "Ma...really? I haven't seen them in four days."

"Erin, I'm not in the mood for your bullshit today. You give Sadee these special privileges, like I'm not their grandmother too. I should've gotten them first, not her." She started out of the living room. "Whose idea was that anyways? Tone's?" She scoffed. "Seems like he calls all the shots."

I followed after her. "Are you serious right now? Sadee lives on the compound. Our flight left early in the morning and I didn't wanna pull them out of the bed just to drag them into the cold and down the road."

"You should've called me, Erin. I'm your mother, not Sadee. I see what her ass is doing, and I don't like it."

I frowned. "What is she doing?"

"Trying to turn my child and my grandchildren against me."

"Ma...have you been drinking?"

"I'm not playing, Erin." We entered the kitchen.

"Me neither. Are you drunk?" She had to be. Sadee wasn't even the type of person to turn people against one another. It was her idea to drop Sanaa and Toni off with my mom in the first place. My mom had gone longer than four days without seeing my kids before, so I didn't understand where all this animosity was stemming from.

"Sasha and Eli bring the twins over all the time." She stopped at the trash can. "I don't have to beg them to let me be a grandma." She turned sideways and pointed the spoon at me. "You, on the other hand, purposely keep them away from me but let them spend all the time in the world with Sadee's ass."

I stared at the back of her head as she placed dishes in the dishwasher and cursed under her breath.

"I haven't done anything to your spoiled, mean ass. *I* had you, not Sadee."

I turned on my heels and headed for Erica's bedroom because I knew Sanaa was most likely in her bedroom sleep. As I climbed the steps, I bounced Toni, expressing how crazy I'd been without kissing her goodnight these past few days. Once I hit the top, I made my way to the linen closet and grabbed two washcloths to wash off her hands and face. I was busying myself with cleaning Toni off in the bathroom when Erica came and stood in the door.

"She started with you too?" she asked, slipping her arms through her coat.

"What's her problem?"

"I don't know, and I'm not trying to find out. She's been tripping all day. I thought you weren't coming back until tomorrow?"

I dried Toni off with a clean towel, handed her to Erica, and cut the light out. "That was the plan, but I missed my babies."

She nodded. "I'm glad you're back. I was gon' go to Sadee's later and chill with her until my homegirl Anias got off work."

"Lord...did your mama know that?"

She shrugged. "I mean, I mentioned it."

I shook my head as she followed me to her room. I cut the light on and smiled at the sight of Sanaa Kelis Morris, my first real love.

"How long has she been asleep?" I trekked to the bed and took a seat.

"Like an hour and half. She was being real fussy."

Nodding, I pulled her small body into my arms, hugged her, and kissed her face. "Naa-Naa..." I whispered.

She stirred a little.

"Ladybug..." I rocked her, and her eyes opened slowly.

With the same hazel orbs as her father, Sanaa stared at me like I was stranger and then a sluggish grin graced her sleepy face. "Hi, Mommy."

"Hi, baby."

She wrapped her little arms around me and gave me a big squeeze.

"You missed me?"

She nodded slowly, still holding onto me.

"I missed you more." I kissed her forehead. "You ready to go home and see Daddy?"

"Yes..." She yawned.

"Okay, let's put your shoes on." I helped her off the bed and she ran to her purple, high top Van's. Once she had them in hand, she rushed back to me and I helped her put them on. After she was situated, I scooped her up into my arms and started out of Erica's room.

"Watch she start trippin' because I'm leaving even though I've been cooped up in the house for two days." Erica groaned with her Louis Vuitton backpack and Toni in hand.

I chuckled as we descended the staircase.

"Erin, who the fuck is this sitting outside of my house?" my mother said with an attitude, as she stood looking out of the glass screen door.

"Royal, my driver, he's cool," I assured her.

"Driver?" She scoffed. "First Sadee and now you? What do y'all need drivers for?"

"Santonio feels more comfortable with us having one." I went to the hall closet to remove coats and overnight bags.

"What are y'all, hood royalty?" She scoffed.

I ignored her.

"He got you that expensive ass car just for someone else to drive you around. I guess. Your hands and feet work just fine. Eli doesn't need drivers."

"Eli and Santonio aren't on the same level either," Erica replied smartly.

"Tuh." My mother stormed towards the back of the house. "Eli is smart enough not to risk his family's life."

After Sanaa had her coat on and Toni her jumper, I didn't even bother saying good-bye to my mother. We left her house and I had no plans on returning any time soon.

# TONE

"Ma!" I called out as I walked through her foyer.

"In here Tonio!"

I followed the sound of her voice to her den. When I entered, her and my auntie Daisy were putting a puzzle together.

"I thought you weren't coming home until tomorrow." She stood up, smoothed her blouse out, and made her way to me.

"Damn, you ain't happy to see ya young bull?"

She rolled her eyes and pulled me into a hug. "Of course, I'm happy to see you. My lil stinker."

I smacked my lips. "Chill, Ma."

Aunt Daisy laughed. "Awww, I remember that nickname. Come here stinker, give Auntie some lovin.'"

I shook my head as they laughed at my expense.

Aunt Daisy met me halfway for a hug and she gave me a squeeze. "How you been, baby?"

I shrugged. "I'm straight."

She let me go. "Your Auntie Paige ain't the same. If you get some free time go check in on her, okay?"

I nodded.

She sauntered back to her seat at the table and continued to work on the puzzle with Ma Duke.

"Where's Erin?" Ma asked me.

"She went to go get my lil' mamas." I took at a seat at the table. "You ain't been giving Grey a hard time, right?"

Ma Duke sighed. "Santonio, I'm forty-seven years old. I don't need a babysitter."

"He ain't a babysitter, though. He's a bodyguard."

"I don't need it."

"Yeah, you do." I knew moms wouldn't like having a driver, but Grey was the best at what he did. He was a lil older than Ross at thirty-eight, but he was a beast. He would keep moms protected.

"If you say so."

"Sisters!" Aunt Macie called out.

I took that as my cue to bounce. "I'll see you later, lil' lady, a'ight?"

"Tonio..." Ma Duke shook her head. "Don't do that."

I placed a quick kiss on her forehead and prepared to leave.

"What y'all in here doing?"

I walked past her.

"Well hello to you too, nephew."

"Sup."

"Tell Roman to call me. That little bitch he's with answered the phone so I know she won't deliver the message."

"Now, Macie..." Ma Duke stood up. "I can't let you disrespect Ava. She's family too."

I chuckled. "This bitch is crazy."

"Santonio!"

"Ma, why the fuck do you keep coming to this bitch's rescue?"

"Nephew...take a walk," Aunt Daisy said sternly. "Don't disrespect your mother just because your auntie is trippin'."

"I'm tired of every fuckin' body in this family ganging up on me!" Macie yelled.

"Oh, shut the hell up Macie!" Aunt Daisy jumped in her face. "I sit back and let you constantly disrespect my sister, and don't say a damn thing, but it stops today!"

"Daisy, please." Ma Duke pulled her back. "This is not how we handle things. Don't stoop down to her level."

Macie chuckled bitterly. "You like when people kiss your ass, so shut up, Sadee."

Aunt Daisy pointed her index finger in Macie's face. Her chest rose up and down violently as she glared at her. "You would think since she raised *your* child for you, you would be more appreciative."

"Daisy..."

Auntie ignored Ma Dukes attempt to silence her.

"You fucked her man, had a fuckin' baby by him, ran off and left her to clean up your mess."

*The fuck?*

I looked down at Ma Duke who seemed to be losing her color.

"Dai-Daisy." She held her chest as her breathing picked up.

Aunt Daisy continued. "You walk around like she owes you something, but she doesn't. Do you know how much you broke her!" She pointed at my mother. "She raised two kids by herself after being deceived by two people she loved."

Macie took a step back. "What about me?! I loved Romaine Santino Chauhan too!" She started crying. "I knew him first!"

*The fuck!*

I looked back to Ma Duke, who was crying.

"And he loved me just as much," Macie kept on. "So much that he married me, and we conceived another child." She smirked. "Rome should be...what? Nineteen."

"What?!" Aunt Daisy charged at Macie and started whooping her ass.

"Daisy!" Ma Duke screamed as I held her back, so she wouldn't get hit. "Daisy! Santonio, stop them."

I didn't want to, but when Aunt Daisy started banging Macie's head on the floor, I had to interject.

"You stupid, selfish bitch!" she screamed. "After all we've done for you, Macie?!"

I pulled her off of Macie and bear hugged her. "Auntie!"

"Just like I didn't want Roman, I didn't want Rome's ass either. There was only room for one woman in my husband's life."

"Macie!" Ma Duke shrieked in disbelief.

After hearing that shit, I let Aunt Daisy go.

She started tagging the shit out of Macie's trifling ass.

I faced Ma Duke when she started crying loudly. Her body was shaking violently and sweat was trickling down her forehead. Just as I reached out to grab her, she collapsed onto the floor, hitting her head on the corner of a brass end table on the way down.

## 11

# IF IT AIN'T ONE THING

ERIN

"Yo, E..." Ava didn't even let me say hello.

"What's up?"

"Have you talked to Tone?"

"No, he hasn't made it home yet. Why?" I buttoned Toni's onesie. "Sanaa, I told you to eat that ice-cream downstairs."

Erica walked into my room and hopped into the bed. "Her butt is hardheaded."

"E, you might wanna come to St. Luke's South ASAP. It's Ms. Sadee."

My heart dropped, but I jumped out of the bed. "I'm on my way." I ended the call.

"What's the matter?" Erica sat up.

"Can you watch the girls for me? I'll be right back."

"Of course." She hopped out of the bed. "Is everything okay?"

"I'll keep you updated."

After slipping my feet into a pair of Uggs, I snatched up my purse and rushed out of the room.

*God, please let her be okay.*

I blinked, and a lone tear slipped from my eye and slid down my cheek.

~

Royal put the truck in park, hopped out the car, and opened my door. I couldn't move, though. I was too terrified of entering the hospital and finding out something tragic had happened to Sadee. The tears wouldn't stop falling, and even though it was freezing outside, Royal shut the door and stood quietly outside the door until I could pull myself together. Taking a deep breath, I slipped on my crossbody bag and tapped twice on the window.

"You okay?" Royal helped me out of the car.

I nodded.

The moment I entered the hospital, I saw Ava walking down the hallway.

"Av!" I called out to her.

She spun around and her doleful eyes made me stop in my tracks. She sighed and then switched in my direction. "Hey, E. Everybody's upstairs."

"Is she okay? What happened? Where's Santonio?" I refused to cry again, so I stopped rambling and took a deep breath.

"She passed out and hit her head on the way down. Tone's upstairs. She has a concussion. She woke up for a little while, but then crashed again."

I nodded as we made our way to the elevators.

"E, before she passed out..." Ava looked down at the coffee cup in her hand. "Daisy told Tone that Roman and Santonio were brothers."

I stared at her profile. "*What?*"

"They have the same daddy." She shook her head. "I should've known that story about her friend was really about her. I should've put two and two together."

"So..."

"Macie had Roman, left him with Sadee, and ran off with their daddy."

My heart immediately went out to Sadee.

*Damn.*

"But that's not even the kicker..."

We stepped onto the elevator.

"They have a little sister named Rome."

My eyes grew big. "Macie has a daughter?"

"Yep." Ava pressed the button to take us to the floor Sadee was on. "She's nineteen. Macie gave her up for adoption."

"Wow. I knew Macie was trifling, but damn."

"Daisy whooped her ass."

I shook my head in disbelief as we got off the elevator.

"Poor Sadee is really going through a lot, yo." Ava sighed.

We made our way down the hall quietly. I knew a million questions were running through Santonio's head. Like why hadn't Sadee told him. Did she ever plan to? Knowing Sadee, she hadn't said anything to keep peace within the family. But I knew Santonio, and he wouldn't look at it like that.

When we stepped into the waiting room, Roman was sitting alone, staring down at the floor. Ava made her way to him and sat next to him.

"Baby, drink this." She offered him the cup of coffee.

"Ava..." He didn't even look up. "I told you I didn't feel like being bothered, man."

Ava's face twisted up. "I'm just trying to be supportive, Roman. Why the fuck do you push me away whenever you're going through something?"

"I didn't ask yo ass to be here!" he barked, and Ava jumped a little. "Take yo ass home." Finally, he looked at her with the meanest look on his face. "You gettin' on my fuckin' nerves."

Ava jumped up from her seat and threw the cup of coffee across the room. "Bet! Fuck you, yo!" She stormed past me.

"Nah, fuck you!"

"Ro..." I was shocked Roman was coming at Ava like this.

"Aye E, no disrespect, but stay outta my fuckin' business."

"Who the fuck you talkin' to, nigga?" Hearing Tone from behind me made me turn around.

"Baby..." I hurriedly made my way to him.

"Nigga, I was talkin' to Erin." Roman got up from his seat.

"Excuse me, you guys are going to have to take this outside, or I'm calling security." The nurse at the nurses' station came around the corner and looked down at the mess Ava had made.

"Santonio." I hugged his body. "Don't do this." I gave him a tight squeeze. "You and Ro are just upset right now. Sadee wouldn't want y'all fighting while she's down." I found myself getting choked up. "Please, just walk away. Take me to see her."

His body stayed tight, but I knew he was contemplating everything I had just said.

I held on tighter. "That's your brother. Don't say or do anything you gon' regret later, baby."

"Man, fuck this shit," Roman said before I heard footsteps pass by us.

I released Santonio and stared up at him. His hazel eyes were dark and scary. "Don't take your anger out on Roman. He's already taking his out on Ava."

He nodded in understanding.

"Thank you." I grabbed both sides of his face, pulled his head downwards, and kissed his cheek.

In return, he picked me up and I wrapped my legs around his waist. He hugged me tightly and placed his face in the crook of my neck.

"She had to get stitches." His embrace tightened. "It was so much blood, E. I thought..."

I hugged his neck. "Baby, she's a strong woman. She's going to be okay. They're going to take care of her. And when she's released, she'll come home with us."

He nodded, face still in my neck. I'm sure to the people passing by we looked crazy as hell, but if my baby needed to be comforted, then I was going to do just that.

"So, you and Ro are brothers?" I turned the Balenciaga cap on his head backwards.

"Yeah...same pops. Crazy, right?"

I chuckled. "Yeah. I mean, y'all do favor each other...*a lot*." But just like everybody else, we all just assumed it was because their mothers were sisters. The only difference in their appearances were Santonio's eyes, Roman's long hair, and their build. Ro was built like a basketball player and Santonio like he played football.

"I got lil a sister too." He walked us to a free seat and sat down with me in his lap, our fronts facing.

"Rome..." I stroked his beard. "Ava told me."

"Shit is wild."

"That's just one more thing we have in common." I kissed his nose. "We both have two daughters."

He chuckled.

"One brother and one sister." I smiled.

Santonio gave my ass a firm squeeze. "I guess you right."

"Oh..." I snapped. "And we're both pretty good in bed."

He smacked his lips. "You a'ight."

"You weren't saying that in Arizona, nigga." I smirked. "I had them toes pointed."

He laughed. That dimple sunk into his cheek and my smile grew wider.

"Where's Sanaa and Toni?" He caressed my thighs.

"At home with Erica."

He frowned. "You left them in a empty crib, E? Call Erica and tell her to go to the main house."

I shook my head. "They're already there. I said they were at *home*."

He licked his lips, eyeing me.

"I rushed here as soon as Ava told me moms was here. I wanna see her. Even if she's not awake, I want her to know I came." Sadee was a mother figure to me. Had been for a long while. I needed to see her with my own eyes. Kiss her cheek and pray over her.

"A'ight." Santonio pecked my lips. "Come on."

# TONE

The only thing that saved Roman from getting his ass beat was the sad look in Erin's eyes right before she wrapped her arms around me. I could tell she had been crying. Making sure she was straight was more important than putting Ro through a wall. That, and I had heard how he talked to Ava. My little brother was confused and hurt. We both were.

I never suspected we were brothers. We had the same last name as everybody on our mothers' side. Yeah, we had a lot of similarities, but Drake favored us too. Did that mean he was our brother as well? Shit, most of my female cousins looked like *they* could be sisters. Now I was looking at everybody differently.

While Erin sat in the room with Ma Duke, I chilled in the waiting room. When my phone started ringing and I saw it was Don Capporelli calling, I sucked my teeth.

"Don..."

"Santonio. How are you?"

"I've been better."

He chuckled. "I will be expecting you in Portland tomorrow evening."

I stared at the wall.

"There is matter of...eh...*agitazione*."

*Turmoil.*

"I will see you tomorrow, Santonio." And with that, he hung up.

Hearing the elevators ding, I glanced up to see Grey exiting. I leaned back in my chair as he approached me.

"Mr. Morris."

"Grey." I nodded.

"How is your mother?"

"She's doing better."

He stood there for a moment. "Okay, well when she wakes tell her we've been praying for a speedy recovery at the church." Grey fixed the sleeves on his tailored Armani suit.

"'Preciate that." I got up, dapped him, and pulled him into a quick embrace. "I'll let her know."

"No problem." He looked down the hall then back at me. "You got anybody guarding her room?"

"Yeah. Ross and Smoke are down there."

Grey checked the time on his Rolex. "You mind if I have word?"

"About?" I stared at him.

"Protocol and safety. Smoke had a mishap earlier this week. I just wanna rap wit' em."

I nodded and retook my seat.

"Shouldn't take long." Grey made sure his gun was hidden before taking off.

When me and E got home, it was well after midnight. We both trekked up the right side of the grand staircase quietly. Even though the house was big, Sanaa had a way of knowing whenever we were near. When we made it to our bedroom, I took a seat on the bed and E switched to the en-suite bathroom. I tossed all three of my phones onto the bed, laid back, and closed my eyes. I had officially been up for over twenty-four hours.

"Are you getting in the shower?" I looked over and E was standing in the door way in just a pair of sheer orange panties.

"Yeah, here I come." I closed my eyes until my burner phone sounded off.

*The fuck this bitch want?*

I stared at Xenia's name. Ignoring her call, I got out of bed and went to join my love in the shower. As soon as I stepped inside, my dicked swelled from the sight before me. There E stood, eyes closed, head back, letting the water from each shower head rain down on her. In a daze, I stood mesmerized at the mother of my kids and the love of my life. I loved the lil' pudge in her stomach and the stretch marks on her ass my daughters had given her.

I scared her when I came behind her and wrapped my arms around her soft body. No words were exchanged. I held onto her and rocked from side to side slowly. She spun around to look at me and I swept her hair from off her face. When she wrapped her arms around my neck, I lifted her body and sat her down on my dick. Her gushy center sucked me in, almost making my knees buckle.

I held onto Erin's waist as I slid her up and down my dick.

"Yes, baby..." she whispered into my lips. "Fuck this pussy." She started throwing that muthafucka back.

"Lil' freaky ass." I pounded harder.

"Mmm..." she moaned before shoving her tongue in my mouth.

I grabbed two handfuls of her ass and made sure hit to the bottom of her pussy with every thrust.

*Knock, knock.*

"Mommy..." Sanaa's lil' squeaky voice broke my concentration.

"Don't stop, baby." E didn't miss a beat. "Harder, baby."

*Knock, knock.*

Erin started grinding, matching my strokes. "I want you to cum with me..." Her sexy, sultry voice did something to me.

"Fuck." I whimpered like a lil' bitch. But I wasn't ashamed. I could be open with Erin.

*Knock, knock.*

"Mommy!"

Erin worked her hips quicker. I knew what she was doing, trying to make me bust faster than I usually did, and the shit was working.

"E..."

She cut me off and we shared a sloppy kiss. That was all it took for me to bust a fat nut. I held onto E's body firmly when her pussy muscles contracted and her legs started vibrating. I muffled her moans with a hard kiss as she came.

*Knock, knock.*

"Daddy!"

~

"Daddy, look!" Sanaa exclaimed excitedly, shoving her iPad in my face.

The bright light made me squint my eyes.

"Sanaa, you're getting ready to go lay back down." Erin snuggled underneath me.

"Why?" Naa pouted.

"Cause Daddy's sleepy." Erin ran her fingers through Sanaa's hair.

"Go to sleep." Sanaa jumped on top of us, giggling.

Her laughter got louder when I started tickling her sides.

"Good, it's a family reunion." Erica stood in the doorway with Toni. "Take this." She laughed.

"Don't treat my baby like that." Erin snickered. "Come on, mama," she cooed, and Toni's little spoiled ass started whining. Erin scooted to the edge of the bed and grabbed Toni from her.

"Quit frontin' for your mama." Erica plopped down and made herself comfortable in our custom bed. It was big enough to fit at least twenty people comfortably.

"Toni-noni," I grumbled with my eyes closed.

"You sleepy, Daddy?" Sanaa asked.

My burner phone went off and I reached into my red Nike sweatpants. "Yeah, Naa-Naa, Daddy's sleepy."

Xenia was calling again.

"Well, I'm out." Erica got up. "E, can I get a few dollars to go to the mall with Anias tomorrow? Eli won't give me any money 'cause I called Sasha a stupid "b" word last week."

Erin sighed. "Erica...really? Why?"

I ignored Xenia again.

"'Cause she is."

Erin shook her head. "Yeah, I'll give you something before you leave."

"Bet." Erica made her way out. "Oh, yeah!" She snapped her fingers and backtracked. "Brother Tone."

I looked at her.

"Can you convince your wife to let me move in?"

I frowned. "Why would I do that?"

"Uh, because y'all would have a in-house babysitter. For a fee, of course."

"Let me get this straight." I chuckled. "I gotta pay you to live with me?"

Her and Erin laughed.

"Ain't that some shit."

"No." She cracked up. "Only when y'all need me to babysit, brother." She giggled.

Sanaa laughed too, not even knowing what was so funny.

"I'll think about it." I shook my head.

"Remember, it takes a village." Erica pranced out, still laughing.

"That girl is silly." Erin chuckled.

I rested my right arm behind my head and closed my eyes. "That's yo sister."

# 12

# KEEP PUSHIN' ON...NO MATTER WHAT

### ERIN

I'm sure a lot of people like my mom, Eli, Sasha and a few others looked down or thought lesser of me because I had taken Santonio back. I didn't care, though. What was done was done, and it is what it is. In life, you have to learn to live with regrets, not in them. And you know who taught me that? Santonio Keith Morris.

I was in the kitchen preparing breakfast when I heard the doorbell. I washed my hands, dried them off, and took off to the front door. Whoever was at the door was persistent because they rang the bell twice more. Santonio wasn't home, but before he left, he swore we would have protection at all times. He also showed me where all the guns in the house were. I grabbed the one in the hall closet and continued my journey towards the front of my home.

"Who is it?"

"Ava."

"And Chance!"

I unlocked the door and pulled one of the huge doors open. "Hey." I stepped to the side. "What y'all doing here this early?"

Chance, who was holding a basket of fruit, waltzed right in and continued down the hall. "This is nice, E!" she called over her shoulder. "I've always wanted to see what the inside of Tone's palace looked like."

My eyes rolled over to Ava. "Sup, Av."

"Hey," she said dryly. "You busy?"

I shook my head as I closed the door. "What's up?

"Girl, nothing. I just dropped Rajon off with his egg donor." She looked around as we headed back to the kitchen. "This is crazy dope, yo." She whistled. "Y'all living like royals for real in this muthafucka."

We stopped so I could put the gun back. "Yeah, Santonio did the most with this."

When Santonio left early this morning, I ventured around to get well acquainted with my new home and had to hand it to him. He spared no expenses. The house was immaculate. My only concern was keeping Sanaa and Toni from hurting themselves on any sharp edges or falling down the grand staircase. I cringed at the thought alone. I was putting up safety guards *asap.*

We reached the kitchen and Chance was standing at the stove. "I'm glad you're cooking breakfast since *somebody* wouldn't let me stop at Burger King." She shot Ava a look.

"Y'all don't have drivers?" I looked back and forth between the duo.

"Yeah, but Ava convinced them to let us drive and they just followed."

Ava shrugged. "What can I say? I'm good with words."

"She threatened to shoot him, he called Roman, Ro tried to get her to get on the phone, and then she threatened to shoot him too." Motor Mouth rambled off as she moved around the kitchen to finish what I had started.

Laughing, I started helping Chance.

Ava took a seat at the island. "I'm done with Roman's ass. He don't appreciate me, so I'm going back to New York."

I stopped laughing. "What?" I hadn't known Ava that long, but I didn't want her to leave. "Av, you're just mad."

"No, I'm fed the fuck up, E." Chance slid a chopping block, a butcher knife, and a mix of different vegetables across the island to her.

"All we do lately if we aren't fuckin' is argue." She sighed sadly. "I know it's because he's going through a lot...I know that. But what about me?"

"Ava, really?" Chance began cracking eggs. "He just lost his cousin, the only mother he's ever known is in the hospital, and he just found out he has a brother he's known his entire life, and a sister that could be anywhere." Chance stopped what she was doing. "I think you should be a little more empathetic."

"Empathetic?" Ava scoffed. "What the fuck you think I've been doing? He's not the only muthafucka going through something, yo. I get that he's hurting. His hurt is mine."

"Just be patient, that's all I'm saying," Chance suggested.

"Like how you are with True?"

My eyes shot up from the pancake batter I was preparing and landed on Ava.

"What is that supposed to mean?" Chance looked like her feelings were crushed.

"You deal with a bunch of bullshit trying to be 'patient,' and the whole time he does whatever the fuck he wants. He fucks who he wants, talks to who he wants, goes wherever the hell he wants, but puts limitations on you." Ava's intense gaze stayed on Chance.

"True isn't my man." Chance's voice cracked. "He's allowed that kind of freedom."

"Not when you're in love with him." Ava smirked. "You loyal to a nigga that don't appreciate the shit you do, but you so *patient* you don't recognize *game*."

"Ava." I stepped in. "So, because Roman is hurting your feelings, you gon' purposely hurt Chance's?" I glared at her. "That's fucked up and you know it."

Ava's piercing gaze landed on me. "Erin, bye. Tone does whatever the fuck he wants too."

I dropped the items in my hands. "Look," I made my way around the island, "I get that you upset. And I'm mad at Roman for you. But what you not gon' do is sit in my shit and disrespect me or Chance because we haven't done shit to you. Take that up with Ro."

I stopped right in front of her.

"Yo, E...get out my face." She mugged me.

"Or what?"

"What y'all down here doing?" Erica entered the kitchen holding Toni. "Sup Av, hey Channy." She smiled. "Y'all need help?"

The room fell silent as me and Ava continued to stare each other down.

"Yeah." We both looked to Chance. "You can make the orange juice." Tears lined the brim of her eyes. "Fresh squeezed is way better than that stuff in a container."

"Cool." Erica beamed. "Let me put Toni in her swing and go see if Sanaa is up." She spun back around to leave. "I'm kickin' it with the big dogs today, Toni."

After she was gone, my eyes rolled back to Chance. She blinked, and a few tears slipped out and rolled down her cheeks. My gaze shifted back to Ava and she hung her head.

"Chance..." She sighed.

I made my way back around the island.

"My bad." Ava's weak ass apology made me roll my eyes. She attempted to clean it up. "I'm sorry."

Chance wiped her face. "It's okay. I know you're going through a lot right now." She sniffled. "Emotions are running high." She smiled. "Don't sweat it, Av."

Ava looked down at the vegetables in front of her. "I'm just stressed the fuck out. Between flying back and forth to New York to check on my shops, handling my brothers' business affairs, Tone's shit, Rajon's stupid ass mama, and the shit that's goin' on with Ro..." She closed her eyes. "I know that don't justify what I said, but you know I fucks with you Chance." She opened her eyes, rose her head, and looked at me. "You too, Erin."

I crossed my arms. "I *know* you got a lot on your plate. You're just as affiliated with the mob as one of the boys. I know that shit can take a toll on you."

She nodded.

"But if you tryna go blow for blow in this bitch, I'm down." I chuckled.

Ava sucked her teeth. "Bitch, I will tase yo ass before I let you dog me like you did that hoe at Swope."

I laughed.

"I'm dead ass. That shit should have been on Worldstar."

Chance chuckled.

"You still love me Channy-pooh?" Ava pouted.

Chance tapped her chin. "I'll let you know later."

We all laughed. Just as we died down, Erica waltzed back into the kitchen. "Sanaa is still sleep." She sat a baby monitor on the counter. "And Toni is in her swing."

"Let me make her a bottle." I went for the cabinets.

"I still can't believe Macie's trif ass." Ava started prepping to cut up vegetables.

I nodded in agreement. "I wonder where Rome is."

"Wait...who's Rome?" Erica asked, opening the refrigerator.

"Roman and Tone's little sister." Ava began chopping tomatoes.

"How can Roman and Tone have the same sister?" Erica removed a bag of oranges. "That's not even possible."

I continued making Toni a bottle. "Because Macie fucked Sadee's nigga and ran off with him."

Erica's mouth dropped in disbelief. "You lying."

"I wish I was."

"That's some Jerry Springer shit right there." Erica shook her head.

"Language." I gave her the side eye and she smacked her lips.

"We should try to find her." Chance finally spoke. "See if she's okay, and if not, send for her to live here."

I nodded in agreement.

Ava sighed. "Can we do that *after* breakfast?"

# TONE

When I stepped off the jet, Kai Money and Javier were waiting for me in the car.

"My guy." I slapped fives with Kai after I shut my door.

"Everything good on the home front?" he asked, passing me a blunt.

I nodded.

"Sup, boss man." Javier's choppy English because of Hispanic accent put you in the mind of 'Baby Joker' from *Next Friday*.

We shared a handshake. "What's good, youngin'." I looked back at Kai Money. "Everything's straight."

He nodded. "The wife wasn't happy about me leaving. Told me I had two days to get back." Kai chuckled.

"Not Blaze." I grinned.

"Don't let lil' mama fool you, my G. Her ass stay bossin' up on a nigga."

Javier laughed. "I'm just happy I ain't gotta sleep wit' one eye open no more, B."

I shook my head. "I know that feeling, trust me."

"That's why I'm never settling down with one." Javier frowned. "These chicas are wild." He took a long drag of the weed.

At twenty-three, Javier was one of the youngest lieutenants on my team. He was a hot head who didn't have shit to lose. No moms, pops, and no immediate or distant relatives. He was a lone wolf. We were all he had so his loyalty ran deep as shit. I'd met him back when me and E took a trip to Cali a couple years ago. He was a beast and even though he was young, niggas where he was from feared him.

"You just ain't met the right one, young bull. It'll happen for you. Watch."

∼

"Ah...Santonio," Don Capporelli greeted with wide arms. "Feels like it's been a long time, no?"

I approached him, and we exchanged handshakes.

"Would you like a drink?" He motioned for his bodyguard to go to the bar.

"Nah, I'm good."

"Santonio." He took a seat at the table and flicked his wrist "Please, sit. I was told you were in company of Xenia Masseria." Don smiled. *"Non è incantevole?"*

"She's a'ight." He'd asked me if I thought Xenia was *lovely.*

"I'm guessing you took care of the liability." Don Capporelli put a cigar to his lips and the guard standing next to him lit it for him.

"I *guess* you could say that." I glanced around the room.

Don chuckled. "Santonio, I expect great things from you. Wonderful things."

Just as those words left his mouth, there was a tap on the door. One of Don Capporelli's men answered and Frank Masseria entered. Xenia followed close behind. When her sultry eyes landed on me, she smirked.

Don Capporelli and Don Masseria shared a brotherly embrace. *"È così bello vederti."*

I stood up to greet both him and Xenia's thirsty ass. "Don Masseria...Xenia." I extended my hand to the both of them one by one before retaking my seat at the table.

"It's good to see you, Dio...and so soon." Xenia smiled.

I nodded.

"Santonio." Don Masseria glanced from Xenia to me and then back to her. "My daughter tells me you two have grown rather close."

I frowned. My eyes bounced to Xenia. "Is that what she told you?"

"I was telling my father we'd come to a mutual understanding in Arizona."

"And what was that?" I titled my head, waiting on her to lie.

"We both agree we will take the Candido Cartel to the next level." She smirked. "The Masseria and Capporellis will take over. Don Lucia and Don Astenello will have no other choice but to hop on board."

"Ah..." Don Capporelli puffed on his cigar.

"Of course, " Xenia shrugged, "some minor adjustments had to be arranged." She glanced at me. "Still do."

I ran my hand across the top of my head.

Don Capporelli's butler walked into the room. "Augusto," Don acknowledged him, and he took off to the bar.

"Xenia and Santonio," Don Masseria started, "we will make a lot of enemies. But I know there is nothing you two can't handle together."

"Father, I'm sure *together* Dio and I could conquer the world." Xenia ran the tip of her tongue across the inside of her top lip. "Right, Dio?"

"As long as you remember what I said." I wasn't playing when I said I didn't mix business with pleasure. That was the quickest way to get caught up. Bitches like Xenia were all about power and a dollar. She would do anything to get to the top, even if she had to fuck and suck her way there. That and me promising Erin I would do right by her this go 'round. After fighting for so long, I had my family, and I wasn't risking that for the nobody.

Xenia rolled her eyes.

"Shall we discuss the situation with Bruce?" Don Masseria looked around the table.

"I'd rather not." Don Capporelli stared down at the rings on his right hand.

Don Masseria nodded.

Augusto placed a glass in front of me. I nodded my appreciation.

"My son unfortunately had to be taught a lesson. I did my best to school him." Don Capporelli puffed his cigar twice. "I will leave it at that."

Xenia sipped from her glass.

"I've always had a son in you, Santonio. I trust you with my last name." Don raised his glass.

"'Preciate that, Don." I rose my glass in recognition.

I'd always been a hot-headed nigga. To be honest, I should've been dead by now. I had jumped into this lifestyle head first, with a one motive: get money. I had been through a bunch of shit, seen a lot of people die. Bodied plenty. It would be a miracle and a blessing for me to make it out alive.

I didn't count on it. In all honesty, I was shocked as fuck when I turned thirty this year. I'm not scared to die; never had been, never will be. I welcome that shit with open arms. Cause in reality, I felt like we were already living in hell, so I could bank on death being easy.

"To the Candido!" Don Masseria held up glass up.

"To the Candido..."

"You can't avoid me forever, Dio." Xenia stood next to me in the elevator.

After a few drinks, I respectfully let Don Capporelli know I would see him in a couple hours. As I made my exit, Xenia jumped up from her seat at the table and followed me out of the room.

"Xenia, shorty, are you hard of hearing?" I stared down at her. "You fine, baby, but you not dope enough to take me away from my wife."

I faced forward.

"So, you're married?" she asked, confused.

I nodded.

"She doesn't look like the type of woman that could hold your attention for long." The amusement in her voice caused me to look at her again. "You seem like a man that needs something a little more exotic."

I chuckled.

"She looks angry. That kind of energy can rub off on you, you know." She rubbed my arm. "You need a woman that'll go to war with you, not against you."

I licked my lips. "Trust, E gon' go to war with me *and* for me. With whoever, whenever, however."

Her head snapped back, and a mug formed on her face. "Is that right?"

"Sho nuff." I shook my head. Chicks like Xenia made it hard for niggas to stay faithful. Bitches with no self-respect throwing themselves at you on the daily *knowing* you had a woman but not caring were the reason niggas got caught the fuck up. I wasn't going out like that, though.

The elevator dinged, and I let her step off first. We walked in complete silence the entire way to the entrance. Xenia made sure to swing her hips extra hard, making her ass vibrate in that tight ass skirt. When we got to the exit, our drivers were waiting for us. We went separate ways, and just when I was about to hop in the whip, Xenia called my name.

Holding onto the door, I looked her frame over and then stared into her eyes. "Wassup?"

"What do you see in her?"

I tugged at my beard. "My future."

# 13

# SAY HELLO TO THE BAD GUY

ERIN

E ven though Sadee was out of the hospital, I was still concerned about her well-being. Well, more so her mental state. Her husband and her sister had dogged her out in the worst way. Not only was she stressed but she was dehydrated too, which was why she'd passed out. The doctor gave her the okay to go home a day ago and she had been staying with me and the kids.

Santonio still wasn't back from Portland, but he called every morning and FaceTimed every night. He looked tired and even though he smiled and joked with us, I could see the pain in his eyes. I wanted him home. Wanted to him to spend a day relaxing, catching up on sleep. He'd been moving around a lot, but I understood the hustle and grind were the reasons we were able to live the way we did.

I was spoiled. His mother, his daughters, most of the women in his family...were spoiled. And he didn't do it out of obligation. Santonio took care of us because he wouldn't have it no other way. He had a lot of people depending on him. He paid several different house and car notes, medical bills, and even took care of his little cousins—some that he hadn't seen in months. Santonio was hard, but he looked out for anybody he cared about.

Christmas was coming soon, and I hoped he didn't plan on being gone for the holidays. I hadn't come to a final conclusion, but I wanted to celebrate the holiday here in our home. Of course, with only close family and friends. Santonio would have a fit if I invited anyone outside of our immediate family. He didn't play about where he laid his head.

I was lying in the bed with Toni doing some last-minute online Christmas shopping when my phone sounded off. Seeing it was Sasha, I almost didn't answer, but my dumb ass did anyway.

"Yeah?"

"E?"

"Mmhm..." I massaged Toni's scalp gently.

"How you been?"

"Okay."

The line went silent for all of ten seconds, and then...

"Erin, we need to have a heart to heart."

I frowned. "Do we?" I had tried to have a conversation with Sasha. More than once.

"Yes, really." I heard the attitude in her deliverance.

"About what? Why you fucked my brother, got pregnant, lied, and then tried to blame me for him being a ain't shit nigga?" I flipped through the channels to find something to watch.

"E, quit acting like your shit don't stink."

I chuckled.

"You hurt my feelings and I hurt yours. That don't make it right, but we're even. You've done things to make me question our friendship and I'm sure I've done the same."

"Sasha, I tried to get down to the bottom of why you were so angry. I don't care now."

"Why? Because you're back with Tone? After what he did to Eli?"

I scoffed. "No, because I don't wanna keep going back and forth with you. All we're doing is placing the blame on the other person." At the end of the day, when you pointed a finger, three more pointed back at you. I wasn't trying to live like that.

"'Cause you won't admit that you're wrong. Why would you

continue to mess with the same man who had something to do to
with what happened to Nette?"

"Why you fuck my brother and get pregnant?"

"Wow. E, you've changed."

"Most people do over time."

Sasha sighed. "We used to talk about everything. Ever since
you've started back dealing with Tone, nothing is the same."

"That's a lie and you know it. Even when you acted like a bitch
and constantly came at me sideways, I still treated you like a sister."
When I noticed Toni was asleep, I made sure she was comfortable.
"Everybody makes mistakes, Sasha. There are a lot of things I've done
that I'm not proud of, and I'll take ownership. You need to do the
same. I never switched up on you, even when you did some fucked
up shit."

"Like?"

I wanted to put my hand through the phone and backhand her
dumb ass.

"E, you chose a man over Nette. You cut everybody off for a while
too when y'all broke up. You smiled in my face and faked like you
were okay with what me and Eli were doing, which is probably why
you didn't tell me about him still fuckin' both of his baby mamas.
Then, Tone tried to kill your blood brother and he disrespected your
mother." She tried to read me. "But you walk around like you don't
know why I'm so bothered."

"Sasha, you're judgmental as fuck for somebody who has plenty
of skeletons in their closet." I sat up straight. "You had two men
thinking they were the twins' daddy. You lived in my house, rent free,
and I offered you and the babies y'all own room." I got upset. "You
keep pointing out every wrong thing I've done, but what about my
good?" I got choked up. "What about my sacrifices?"

"What about mine?!"

"You're self-centered, Sasha." I chuckled. "You need help. Your
baby daddy got all that money, tell him to get your head checked."

She scoffed. "When I find a doctor, I'll text you his number."

"You do that. Until then, you have no reason to contact me. I still owe you an ass whoopin.' I ain't forgot." And with that, I hung up the phone.

Taking a deep breath, I exhaled slowly. I was proud of myself. Sasha was trying to knock me off my square. I had more important things going on in my life. Time was money, and something I could never get back, so I couldn't afford to keep arguing with her ass. It was no secret that misery loved company. I wasn't about to let Sasha's depressed ass bring me down to her level.

I had real problems. Real stress. Real shit happening. She hadn't called me to make amends, she was still blaming me for shit I had no control over. What *did* fuck with me, though, was how she could always forgive Eli every time he screwed up.

Where was my forgiveness? Where was my understanding? Where the fuck was my compromise? I now knew I would never get either of those. So, I wasn't giving them.

Just as I relaxed, a call from my mother came through. I rolled my eyes and ignored her. She called twice more and then texted.

**Mom:** *I know you see my calling you Erin*

**Me:** *I'm busy*

**Mom:** *Call me now*

**Me:** *I just said I was busy*

She called me, and I pressed ignore.

**Mom:** *Don't ask me for shit else Erin. Ima remember this*

I stared at the message.

**Mom:** *At least I know I got Eli. He never turned on his back on me.*

**Mom:** *When that nigga breaks your heart don't call me!*

My shoulders dropped. I went to my call log and was about to press on her name when she texted me again.

**Mom:** *I hope Sanaa and Toni don't grow up to be like you*

I tossed my phone and snuggled next to Toni. I stared at her as I ran my hands through her soft hair. She looked so peaceful with her favorite Winnie the Pooh pacifier in her mouth. I closed my eyes and warm tears slid down the bridge of my nose and landed on my pillow case. I held Toni tighter, and concentrated on falling asleep.

# TONE

"Hi, son."

"'Sup, Ma Duke." I stroked my beard. "How you feelin', lil lady?"

"Much better." She sighed. "How are you?"

"I'm straight."

"Tonio..."

I leaned back in my seat.

"I know you probably have a thousand questions you want to ask."

"Nah, not for real. Only one."

"Which is?"

"Why didn't you tell me?" Me and Ma Duke usually talked about everything. We'd had plenty of uncomfortable conversations when I was growing up. Her end went quiet, so I pulled the phone away from my ear to make sure she was still on the line.

"I was embarrassed, Tonio. And, after a while, I just pushed it to the back of my mind. When I realized Macie wasn't coming back, I didn't see any reason to cause confusion in my home." She cleared her throat. "You and Roman treated each other like brothers anyway so I let sleeping dogs lie, baby."

I shook my head.

"Macie was gone for twenty plus years. What she did affected Roman a great deal. He didn't have neither one of his parents. The last thing I wanted to do was upset him anymore."

I clenched my jaw.

"I did what was best."

"For Roman?"

She sighed. "Santonio, you know that's not what I mean."

I stood and went to stand at the balcony door of the penthouse I had been staying in since I arrived in Portland.

"You had a mother who was there every day. He didn't."

"You sure about that?" I challenged. "Seemed to me like Ro had more of a mama than I did."

"That's not fair, Tonio. You had me. And I had enough love to give to the both of you."

I watched the snow fall. "A'ight."

"How is Roman? I tried calling him and he sent me to voicemail."

"I don't know." I hadn't spoken or seen Ro since the hospital. He was acting like a big ass kid, but I wasn't about to babysit his feelings.

"You need to make sure he's alright, Santonio. What Macie did has caused him a lot of hurt. She abandoned him. Finding out you have a brother and a sister in one day is a lot for a person to take on."

I tugged at my beard. "Yeah...I know."

"If I know Roman, he's trying to push Ava away. She called me today sounding real upset."

"That ain't my problem."

"Santonio, I know you're upset too, but you're mentally and emotionally stronger than a lot of people. Help him through this, baby."

Who was gon' help me? Erin? She was going through her own shit. She'd told me about how her mama and the rest of her family was acting because she took me back. My baby had enough on her plate, and I refused to add to it.

"Tonio, did you hear me?"

"Yeah..." I stared down at the snow-filled streets. "I got you."

"Thank you." She yawned.

"No problem, lil' lady." I turned my fitted forward and walked away from the window. "I'ma get wit' you later. Get some sleep."

"Okay, I love you. Don't you ever forget that, okay? I know I'm not the epitome of what a perfect mother should be, but I try. You know that, right?"

"Yeah."

"Okay, I'll call you later."

When she hung up, I paced the floor. I wasn't mad at Ma Duke for looking out for Roman. She'd raised him. She had watched him grow from a boy into a man. Being a mother figure to him came naturally.

Plus, he was there for her when I was young and wild running the streets, when I got locked up, and when I moved to Florida for a while. They had a tight knit bond that was formed off trust and dependency. I would never knock Ma Duke for stepping in and making sure he felt loved. To know she did that shit with a broken heart but didn't take it out on him made me respect my mama that much more. I was proud; I always knew my lil' lady was tough.

My phone sounded off and Roman's name flashed across the screen. It was like the little nigga knew we were talkin' about him.

"Yo..." I took seat on the sectional, tossed my arm over the back of it and relaxed. "Wassup, baby boy."

"Shit."

I nodded. "So, what the fuck you want?"

"Just because you big bro don't mean I won't shoot yo ass." He chuckled.

I smirked. "You good?"

"Yeah man, I'm straight. You?"

I shrugged. "You done throwing tantrums and shit?"

Roman laughed. "Fuck you."

"Nah, you need to go fuck on your woman before she leave yo ass."

He smacked his lips. "Ava Lane ain't going nowhere. She just mad at a nigga right now. She been staying wit' Chance."

I nodded. "Yeah, I know. She called me today to talk business and Chase's bad ass was in the background wreaking havoc."

"That lil' nigga." I knew Roman was shaking his head at his Godson.

True's son, Chase, was bad as fuck. He was only six, but he was a destructive lil' muthafucka. He got suspended from school not too long ago for fighting, and True wouldn't let him leave from in front of the house because of it. Since he couldn't go past the grass, he collected a bunch of rocks and threw them at anybody who passed the house using the sidewalk. Lil' nigga was throwing rocks at old ladies and shit.

"She also told me her, Erin, and Chance were going try to find Rome and reach out to her. She asked for my permission because she knows what kind of lifestyle we live." Ava was smart. She always took necessary precautions.

"Ah, yeah? She didn't tell me that. She called me to say, 'Fuck you, I'm moving back to New York,' and then banged on me."

I laughed.

"I'ma give her crazy ass one more day then I'm going to collect. She bringing her ass back home. I don't care about none of that rah-rah shit she on. Shorty know what's up."

"I hear you."

"But, do you think that's a good idea? To reach out to Rome? What if she don't wanna be contacted? Macie said she was nineteen. If she gave a fuck, she would've been and tried to find her bloodline."

I took my hat off and sat it down next to me. "Like I told Ava, go ahead and do it. If they get in touch with her and she don't wanna be bothered, then leave her the fuck alone." I also told Ava to make sure she had everything she needed. Even if Rome didn't wanna fuck with us, I couldn't have my baby sister out there down bad.

"A'ight cool. You still on the coast?"

"Yeah, I'm leaving tonight. Wassup?"

"Just checkin.' I don't trust them niggas out there." He paused. "If I don't hear from you by tomorrow afternoon, I'm catching a flight." His tone hardened.

I chuckled. "Ah, ain't that cute."

He smacked his lips.

"You worried about your big bro?" I laughed.

"Fuck nah. If something happens to you, who the fuck I'ma beat out on the court once a week? Soft ass nigga." He grumbled and then hung up on me.

Shaking my head, I dropped my phone next to me and laid my head back against the couch. When I got back to Kansas City, I was gon' convince E to spend the holidays on vacation. A nigga needed a temporary break from life. My 2018 had been so up and down, I felt like I was losing my mind. I wanted to bring in my 2019 somewhere out of the country, fuckin' my woman outside under the moonlight.

The knock on the door made me open my eyes and frown. I stood up, removed my piece from my waist and swaggered towards the front of the penthouse. Once I made it to the door, I looked out the peephole and smacked my lips when I saw it was Xenia's retarded ass. I tucked my burner back in my jeans, unlocked the door and pulled it open. I looked Xenia over slowly.

"Wassup, shorty."

She untied the belt to the trench coat she was wearing and revealed her naked body. My dick bricked instantly. Xenia's body was tight—big, perky titties, a flat stomach with a belly button piercing, and a pretty shaved pussy. I grabbed my mans through my pants and licked my lips.

"Hello, Dio," she purred.

# 14

# PRESSURE

ERIN

C hristmas Day...
Santonio tried to convince me to let him take me and the girls to Greece for Christmas and the New Year. After going back and forth for a while, we compromised and decided to go the last week of January for three weeks. He also agreed to let me host the holidays at our house, which was why our home was filled with family and our closest friends. Santonio and I sat on opposite ends of a table that was currently sitting twenty people.

The noise level in the dining room was a mixture of laughter, kids arguing, and grown-up conversation. We'd hired caterers to serve us. The food was delicious, and the drinks were strong as hell. Every now and then, I would catch Santonio staring at me. He would shoot me a quick side smile and then continue talking to his cousin Drake or tend to Toni who was sitting in his lap acting like a brat. No one from my family was here other than Erica, and even though I was a little bothered, I didn't feel out of place.

Skyy went back to Texas after our Arizona trip, and Eli and my mother got my invitations but hadn't replied to my calls or texts. My grandpa promised to drop by, and my grandmother spent twenty minutes on the phone cursing me out, calling me ungrateful. Being with Santonio was causing a rift between my family and me. But my mind was made up. I loved him, and if they loved me, then they would accept that.

The clinking of a glass made me and everyone else look to Santonio. He stood up with Toni still in arms and glanced around the table. Everyone began wrapping up their conversations and after Rajon and Chase stopped arguing, the table got quiet.

"I just wanna say I appreciate everybody coming out today." Santonio bounced Toni. "This is my first Christmas with my family all in one spot." He looked down at Toni. "Family is all we truly got in this world. And whether you're blood related, or not...if you're sitting at this time right now, know I got you."

I smiled.

"Which is why," he stared at me, "when I ask E to marry me, y'all get the first set of invitations."

Everyone started murmuring amongst one another. Me, I almost choked on the wine I had just swallowed.

"Erin," Santonio licked his lips, "come here, baby."

My ass stayed planted right on the cushioned seat. Erica, who was sitting to the left of me, bumped my leg under the table. I looked around the table and everybody had their eyes on me.

"Daddy said come here, Mommy." Sanaa called me out in her squeaky little voice.

My eyes shot back to Santonio. He had that sexy smirk on his face, waiting on me.

I pushed my chair back and stood up. Nervously, I made my way around the table and to Santonio. I could feel my heart rate speed up, and a slight ringing in my ears. My body got hot, and my breathing slowed.

*He's not about to do what I think.*

I stopped in front of Santonio, looked up at him, and then looked away shyly when he winked at me.

"Erin," he gripped my chin and made me look into his eyes, "I love you."

*I know that.*

"I know shit with us been up and down."

I knew that too. I was sure everybody at the table did. He could've said that from across the table. Why would he make me get up? I didn't like all the attention we were receiving.

"You and my daughters mean everything to me, shorty. Even though I'm a fuck up—"

"Awww..." Sanaa cooed from the other end of the table.

Tone chuckled and a few other people laughed.

"I'm sorry, Naa-Naa." He held his hands up in a mock surrender.

"It's okay, Daddy."

Santonio looked back down at me. "I appreciate you for rockin' with me and for having my shorties. You hold a nigga down even when you probably shouldn't." He pinched my cheek and then licked his lips. "It took me almost losing you for a nigga to come to his senses."

I nodded.

"So..." He went into his pocket and removed a red, suede ring box.

"Awww!" Chance squealed.

"Tone..." I took a step back.

"E..." His gaze softened. "Marry me."

"Santo—"

"Ma, hear me out."

I sighed.

"A nigga tryna spend the rest of his life with you. I know I don't have a clean track record, but I swear on my life, right here, right now, that I'ma be better than I was. When I said I wanted my family back, I wanted to come home, but I also wanted you to be my wife. I want you to have my last name."

Tears pooled in my eyes.

*Santonio wants to get married...to me.*

"Nigga was up all night, nervous than a mutha—" He looked to Sanaa. "Than a mug."

I chuckled through sniffles.

"Baby, you the best thing that ever happened to me. I know that might sound cliché, but I get it now. God was looking out for a nigga when He blessed me with you."

He reached out, grabbed me by the front of my shirt, and pulled me closer to him. "I wanna spend my life wit' you, E. Marry me."

I wiped my face gently.

Santonio passed Toni to Drake. He then grabbed my hand, got down on one knee, opened the box, and looked up at me.

"You rockin' wit' me or what E?" His pleading eyes sent my emotions into overdrive.

Tears streamed down my face as I looked down at him, uncertain of what I should do. I loved Tone. We had been through so much. Shit, I was still putting the pieces of my broken heart together. What if he hurt me again? Embarrassed me after I said yes?

I looked to my left and my eyes roamed around the table. Everyone was still; it seemed as though even the kids were anticipating my answer. My blurry gaze rolled back down to Santonio. He looked nervous as tiny specks of sweat formed on his forehead. His palm was sweaty too, and I even noticed his breathing seemed a little labored. I licked my lips, swallowed, and exhaled slowly.

"Baby," Santonio said in a near whisper, "I ain't gon' let you down. I promise." He kissed the back of my hand. "I need you to rock with me."

Warm tears continued to slide down my cheeks as I thought about what I was about to do. I closed my eyes and asked God to guide my path from this point forward.

"Yes." I opened my eyes and a look of relief flushed over Santonio's entire being. "I'm rockin' wit' you."

He cheesed, and that dimple ignited a flame deep down in my soul. Santonio removed the biggest diamond ring I'd ever seen out of the box and slipped it onto my finger. He rose and pulled me into a hug, squeezing me tightly, as everyone at the table clapped and cheered.

"I love you." He rested his forehead against mine and wrapped his hands around my neck.

"I know." I hugged his body. "I love you too."

# TONE

She said yes. The dopest person I had ever known wanted to be my wife. When I stopped by my jeweler's before I came home from Portland, I knew I wanted to get her some new ice. I planned on getting a necklace, some new earrings, maybe even a new charm to add to her bracelet. But when Genesis brought out the rings, it was like a nigga had a epiphany or some shit. I spent over two hours going through his inventory before I found the right one. It was an eight carat, double halo diamond ring.

I had bought E plenty of rings, but this one was different. This one would tie her to my life for eternity. With this one, she would soon have my last name. As I stared across the table at her grinning with Ma Duke, Ava, Chance, and Erica surrounding her, a sense of pride surged through my veins. Erin Kincaid was about to be my wife.

*Damn.*

"I still can't believe you bossed up like that." Roman chuckled.

Que nodded in agreement. "Erin deserves it."

She did. That and much more. And I had every intention on making sure she got whatever she wanted.

Ma Duke stood and tapped a butter knife against her champagne glass a few times. Once she had everyone's attention, she cleared her throat.

"Santonio." She smiled at me. "I've watched you grow from my little stinker," everybody laughed, "to a very strong, bright, giving, loving, and...a little overprotective," she chuckled, "young man. Words can't even begin to express the respect I have for you, son. I just want to say on behalf of everyone here, thank you for having us today. Thank you for the meal, the gifts, and for going out of your way. I'm so proud to be your mother, Tonio. But even prouder..." She looked to E. "That you chose an amazing young woman to mother your children and to give your last name."

She held her glass up. "So, here's a toast to you and Erin. May the lord continue to bless you and watch over you, baby. Mama loves you."

"Cheers." Everybody called out.

"I love you too, Ma." I nodded.

"I love you too, Granny."

Ma Duke laughed. "And Granny loves you and Toni so much more."

An hour later, the dining area was clean, the kids left with Ma Duke, the women went to do their thing, and us men ended up in my "man cave." It was my own little sanctuary. Erin wouldn't even come in even though I told her she could. She felt as though I needed a place where I could be alone to clear my head. Some shit about it being a "healthy confinement."

The space looked more like a bar/pool hall, than a spare room in a house. I was watching Ro kick True's ass in pool when someone started tapping on the door. With my drink in hand, I made my way to it, pulled one of the double doors open, and came face to face with an older man. I only assumed he was older because of his salt and pepper beard and his grey fade. He looked polished in a tailored suit and shiny patent leather dress shoes.

"Wassup?" I eyed him.

He held his hand out. "Santonio?"

I tossed my chin up. "Who you?"

"I'm Evan Kincaid, Erin's grandfather." His hand stayed extended. "It's great to finally put a face with a name, young man."

I accepted his handshake.

"You mind if I have a word with you?" He slipped his hands into his pockets.

I looked behind me and thought against bringing her grandfather into the lion's den. Stepping all the way out, I closed the door behind me and led him to my office in silence. Once we entered, I shut the door, went to my desk, and took a seat on the edge. Mr. Kincaid looked around the room, subtly nodding his head. When his eyes landed back on me, he smirked.

"You've done well for yourself, Santonio."

"Tone." I took a drink from my glass.

"Huh?"

"You can call me Tone."

He nodded.

"What can I do for you Mr. Kincaid?" Erin didn't talk about her family much, but she did express to me how much her grandfather meant to her. They didn't talk all the time, but when they did, they stayed on the phone for hours catching up.

With one hand in his slacks, he pointed at me with his free hand. "I've heard a lot about you, young man." He chuckled. "My grandson says he works with you."

"For," I corrected him. "Eli works *for* me."

Mr. Kincaid nodded. "My daughter isn't quite fond of you."

I shrugged. I didn't like Veronica's unfit ass either. She was part of the reason Erin was so detached from her feelings. I looked up to E, though, because she showered our daughters with love and affection. It didn't matter that she never shared a mother-daughter bond with her own mother. She was attentive as fuck with my lil' mamas.

"And my wife feels as though you've caused a strain in our family."

I stared at him with an emotionless expression. Erin's grandma hadn't even met me before.

"But..." He paused and looked me over. "My granddaughter is madly in love with you."

"I'm madly in love with her too."

He smiled. "I hear congratulations are in order."

I tilted my head. "Oh yeah?"

"Yes, of course. It's not every day a man gets news that one of his favorite girls will be walking down the aisle. So, congratulations, young man."

"'Preciate it." My eyes roamed over to the bar. "You want a drink?"

"Anything dark."

I sat my glass down and swaggered over to the bar.

"My baby seems happy," he stated.

"Erin probably would've been happier if her family would've accepted her invitation so they could've witnessed it." I shot over my shoulder. "Ice?"

Mr. Kincaid chuckled. "I came as soon as could. My wife and the rest of my family aren't too keen of you, Tone." His voice hardened. "And no, dry please."

After making his drink, I walked it to him, and then went back to my desk.

I shrugged. "What can I say." I smirked. "I'm like an acquired taste."

He nodded and then took a drink. "I just want the best and of course safety, for my grandbabies."

"Then you ain't got shit to worry about." I mugged him. "My wife and shorties are good."

Mr. Kincaid stared at me. "You sure about that? I heard you just had a death in the family on Thanksgiving."

I clenched my jaws tight so I wouldn't say some shit to Erin's grandpa that would have me in the doghouse.

"I don't mean to offend you." He took gulp of his drink. "I can look into a man's eyes and see him for who he truly is." He stared at me. "It's an acquired skill."

I smirked.

"I can tell you love my granddaughter, and I can definitely tell she loves you too. Especially to go against her brother for you."

"E didn't go against Eli. He trippin' wit' my baby," I clarified. "Just like she sent an invite for you to come today, she sent one to him and her mama too." I pulled at my beard. "Eli might not ever like me which is cool with me. But E ain't did shit to that nigga or his mama. They're mad at her because she's in love with me. And that ain't gon' change, Mr. Kincaid."

"What do you suppose we do?" He tossed the rest of his drink back.

I shrugged. "I'm all out of ideas."

"I might have one." He walked to the bar and sat his glass down.

# 15

# HOPING TO FIND HOPE

ERIN

"Hey, E." Chance greeted me when I stepped into the room.

The dim lights, soft music, and smell of lavender relaxed me almost instantly. I hadn't spoken to either of them since Christmas, which was three days ago. When we finally did get on the phone, we decided to have the spa day we never had in Arizona.

"Hey, Chance. 'Sup Av." I tightened the rope around the soft, white robe I was wearing.

"What's goin' on, E." Ava lay on her stomach, staring down at her phone through the hole in the table, texting.

"Sorry I'm late." It was time consuming living with a man who found you irresistible. On top of giving baths, picking out wardrobes, doing hair and feeding my girls, I was never done getting ready in a timely manner.

"It's cool." Chance sipped from her water. She sat cross-legged on the massage table, examining her nails. "How are the ladybugs?"

"Spoiled." I chuckled, hopping onto my table. "What y'all been up to?"

"Work," Ava said, still staring at her phone. "I swear, after the New Year I'm going on a two-week hiatus."

Chance giggled. "As long as you text me once a day."

I shook my head. "What about you, Chance?"

"I talked True into letting me open another shop and renovating my loft." She cheesed. "I told him I wanna open up a shop in the city. And that I want it to be my main store. Lee's Summit is cool and all, but I want to be around people that look and act like me."

I nodded in understanding.

"He flat out told me no at first." She rolled her eyes. "But after I came to him with a business plan, design, and I agreed to security, he was game."

"You sure you didn't pout for a week straight?" Ava finally looked up from her phone. "Cause if memory serves me right, you been acting like a brat."

Chance tried to look appalled. Me and Ava laughed at her.

"I wasn't pouting," she said defensively. "I just didn't understand why he wouldn't let me open up a shop when business has been good. And my loft is outdated, so I wanna add a little more space and update my appliances."

"And who's paying for all this?" Ava asked.

I smirked, already knowing the answer.

"True," she said nonchalantly.

"Mmhm." Ava snickered. "Your ass understands why he didn't want you in the city, and your loft is laid the fuck out, yo." Ava gave her the side eye. "Yo ass just don't understand the word 'no.'"

I laughed, nodding my head in agreement. I was sure Chance could afford to open a new building and renovate, but I also knew True would never let her.

"I can't help that my best friend loves me." She shrugged.

*In.*

I smiled at Chance's naive ass.

*Your best friend is in love with you.*

"Whatever you say." Ava rolled her eyes just as the door opened and three women entered the room.

"Good afternoon, ladies." They greeted us and began setting up.

Each woman handed us a towel and told us to remove our robes and get comfortable.

We quickly did what we were told in silence. After we were comfortable, each masseuse found someone's side.

"I found Rome," Ava started.

I stared down at the floor. "That was quick."

"Quit acting like you don't know who I am," she gloated.

"That's great, Av. Where is she?" Chance asked.

"She lives in Minneapolis. Her last name is still the same because she was never adopted." The sadness in Ava's voice tugged at my heart. "Macie's ignorant ass didn't even give her their dad's last name."

Where I was from, sadly, it wasn't unusual for a child to grow up in a single parent home. You either had mommy or daddy, but never both. Or at least if you didn't have mommy and daddy, you had close relatives who were willing to care for you. Not Ava, though and apparently not Rome neither. I knew it played a huge part on the way Ava acted most of the time.

She didn't have parental guidance. Outside of Kai, his people, and now us, Ava didn't have nobody. When she was growing up, birthdays came, but nobody bought her cakes or threw her parties. Holidays like Thanksgiving and Christmas came and went without her making cherishable memories. Thank God she met her people in New York because there would be no telling how she would've ended up. I prayed Rome had some kind of love, *somebody* who cared in Minneapolis.

"I had Tone's lawyer contact her today," Ava continued. "As soon as I hear back from him, I'll let y'all know what's up."

"I feel so bad for her." Chance sighed.

"Don't," Ava snapped. "I'm sure she has had people feeling sorry for her all of her life. She's got the same blood as Ro and Tone running through her veins." She paused. "That alone lets me know she's a tough girl." Ava's voice softened.

The room went silent as we let what Ava said marinate and we enjoyed our massages. I still couldn't believe Santonio and Roman were brothers. I guess it was an easy pill to swallow on behalf of them already acting like siblings. They naturally fell into their new titles. To be honest, I think it made their bond tighter.

Roman called me and apologized about the incident at the hospital before Christmas. I told him I wasn't even tripping, but he insisted on getting that off his chest. However, during that conversation, I did check him about how he treated Ava. He humbly admitted to being wrong and promised to make it up to her. On Christmas, when we weren't opening gifts or eating, they had been all over each other. Ava seemed less tense and more patient as well.

"So, E." Chance broke the silence. "What season are you shooting for?"

"Huh?" I grumbled, damn near falling asleep on the table. The masseuse working on me was most def getting a hefty tip. My shoulders were so knotted from all the stress I'd been carrying on them.

"What season do you wanna get married in?"

"Mid fall."

"That'll be dope," Ava added her two cents. "Fall colors fit you and Tone's relationship perfectly."

"So next fall?" Chance moaned lowly. "This feels so good."

"Or the one after that."

"Good, that'll give me some time to lose weight," she mumbled.

"Don't start that dumb shit," Ava chastised her.

"Whatever." Chance went quiet.

Chance was nowhere near skinny, but she far from fat. She had thick thighs, a big ole butt, and at the most wore a c-cup bra. She complained that her arms jiggled, and her tummy was too squishy. Every other week she was trying a new diet and sometimes went to the gym twice a day. In my eyes, Chance's exterior was just as pure and beautiful as her interior.

"Chance, even if you gained one hundred pounds, you'd still look gorgeous in your bridesmaid dress," I told her.

"You want me to be a bridesmaid?" she squealed lowly.

"Yep. You and Ava." I stared at the floor.

"I went from not ever being to a wedding to being in *two*," Ava stated. I could hear the smile in her voice.

We fell silent again.

"And E..." Chance, of course, broke the silence. "You better not let me ever gain one hundred pounds."

We all laughed. Even the women working on us tried to stifle their chuckles.

"I won't let you go out like that, Chance." I shook my head at her.

# TONE

I put my whip in park and killed the ignition. I glanced at the time on the dash. It was going on four in the evening, and instead of handling shit at my shop, I was sitting outside of Erin's mama's house. I was supposed to have been here by two, but it was hard letting Erin out of the bed in the morning. A nigga had to least get a taste of the pussy. And then of course tear that muthafucka up.

I got out, closed the door and started up the walkway. There was a few niggas hanging outside on the porch. I reached back and pulled the hoodie to the army fatigue jacket I was wearing over my red cardinals fitted cap. When I reached the first step, some cat in a bubble vest stood up. Since my jacket was open, I lifted my white T to warn these niggas not to test my gangster.

"What up, Blood." Bubble coat mugged me.

"Where Mr. Kincaid at?" My eyes shot quickly across every face on the porch. I counted six people. "Go get Mr. Kincaid." I frowned.

Instead of doing what I said, he looked me up and down.

I chuckled.

"Y'all, grandma said..." The screen door swung open and Erica stepped outside. Her eyes landed on me and a smile spread across her lips. "Brother, what you doin' here?"

"Where yo grandpa at?"

Erica looked over her shoulder. "He's in the house playing chess. You need to talk to him?"

"Yeah."

"Come on." She waved for me to come inside.

As I climbed the stairs, I could feel the tension coming from each individual. These niggas knew better than to fuck wit' me, but to some, blood was thicker than water. I was sure they knew what I did to Eli's bitch ass.

When I got inside, I followed Erica through the house.

"I'm surprised to see you here."

I stayed quiet as she led me to the dining room. Mr. Kincaid was sitting at the table, with Eli, playing a game of chess. He must've felt my presence because he looked up at me.

"Tone, I'm glad you could finally make it."

Erica walked back out of the room, mumbling. "I'm calling Erin." She might've thought nobody heard her, but I did.

"Take a seat, young man." Mr. Kincaid gestured to an empty seat at the table.

"Nah, it's cool, OG." I lifted the brim of my hat a little. "I can stand."

"Suit yourself." He shrugged.

Eli stayed quiet.

I smirked, tugging at my beard. "Wassup, E." I tossed my chin up. Other than him copping from me, we didn't exchange words.

He looked back. "What's good, Tone."

"Evan, please go tell your grandsons to pull their pants up over their asses." An older version of Veronica rounded the corner. She looked me up and down and once she was done, her lip curved in disapproval.

"Velma, this is Tone, Erin's fiancé." Mr. Kincaid nonchalantly introduced me.

"Your mother named you *Santonio* and that's what I intend to call you." She glared at me.

I rose my hands in a mock surrender. I didn't want no fonk wit' Granny's old ass. I hadn't come here for all that.

"Velma, I invited Tone over so we could get to know him a little better," Mr. Kincaid stated while concentrating on the chess game. "Young man, you play Chess?"

"Yeah." I only played with Don Capporelli, but a nigga was decent.

"Where is Erin?" Granny smoothed the front of her shirt out.

"She went to the spa."

Granny frowned. "And where are her children?"

"With their grandma."

"That can't be. Veronica isn't here."

I looked at her like she was stupid. Granny was old enough to know everybody had two sides of family. She was trying to piss me off. I broke our stare down and focused back on Mr. Kincaid.

"Velma, Erin's getting married to this young man. Eli," he looked across the table, "did you know your sister was getting married soon?"

Eli shrugged.

Granny scoffed.

I chuckled.

Mr. Kincaid shook his head. "Can we all agree that we want what's best for Erin?" He moved a piece on the board.

"Erin doesn't even know what's best for her. She's been wild since she was thirteen. Grew up too damn fast if you ask me."

Eli's gaze shifted to his grandmother.

"Don't look at me like that, Eli. You know it's true. Erin's been selfish her entire life. She didn't even ask for her mother's blessing." Her eyes shot to me. "Neither did you."

"Didn't know I had to."

Granny's eyes grew big in surprise.

"Velma, stop," Mr. Kincaid said sternly. "He's the father of her children. What did you expect? You should appreciate him wanting to make her an honest woman."

He played his turn.

"Now, in order for their marriage to work, they're going to need support from both his and her side of the family. It can't be one-sided." Mr. Kincaid stared at the board. "I won't let it be one-sided."

"Ev—"

"Velma..." He calmly looked at his wife.

"We need to at least see how Veronica feels about this, Evan."

"Feel about what?" Erin's mama stood in the doorway. "What are you doing here?" She grilled me.

I bit back the need to curse her stupid ass out and cleared my throat. "Me and E getting married."

Veronica grimaced. "No, you're not. Erin didn't talk to me about that."

I shook my head. "Erin is a grown ass woman."

"Young man," Mr. Kincaid jumped in. "I need for you to respect my daughter and my wife."

I swallowed my pride and let him have that.

"Do you see what I mean, Daddy?" Veronica got loud. "Not only is he disrespectful, but he cheats on Erin all the time and he attacked Eli." She snapped. "He better be lucky you're here."

I chuckled.

"I'm asking you to put aside your differences, Veronica. This is who Erin wants to marry. This is who fathered her children, so this young man is family," he said in finality. "Now, me and your mother are getting too old to be concerned when there is no need to be."

Veronica huffed.

"Do you care about your relationship with your daughter, Veronica?" Mr. Kincaid looked at her and then his eyes bounced to his wife. "Velma, don't want your granddaughter to be happy?" His gaze then shifted to Eli. "Your sister is in love.You're not the only man in her life."

"Until he breaks her heart and she's stuck looking stupid," Veronica sneered.

"Veronica, did you not just hear what I said?"

"Yes, Daddy." She looked to Granny for back up.

"Evan, we love Erin. Veronica is just trying to—"

"Velma," Mr. Kincaid cut her off. "We leave tonight. Stop trying to control others' lives from another state. You're not here every day to see firsthand how things go down. Quit babying Veronica and let her mother her own children." He checked her old ass.

"Tone, you're saying you're in love with my baby girl, and I believe you. I could feel the love when I came by on Christmas. All I ask of you is to not put Erin in positions where she has to choose between you and her family."

I nodded. "I can do that."

Veronica sucked her teeth.

I ignored her and made my way toward Mr. Kincaid. "It was nice meeting you Mr. Kincaid."

He stood and extended his hand. "It was a pleasure meeting you as well, young man." We shared a firm handshake. "You take care of my babies."

"No doubt." I stepped back. I had planned on doing that anyways.

# 16

# WHAT YOU GIVE IS WHAT YOU'RE GIVEN...

ERIN

"**W**hat you doin'?" Santonio swaggered into our bedroom taking a bite of cereal.

I removed my glasses and then pushed my MacBook away from me. "I'm making an outline." I watched him as he took a seat on the bed. He looked real chill in navy blue sweats, a white wife beater, black socks and black Nike slides.

"For what?"

"A book."

He looked over his shoulder at me. "Ah, yeah?"

I nodded.

"What's it about so far?"

"Love and Life."

"Those are broad categories." He chewed.

"I know."

"What you got so far?" he asked with his back to me.

"Nothing for real, just a bunch of notes and quotes." I shrugged.

"Let me hear one." He chomped down on another bite.

I reached for my journal, laughing. "You ain't that hungry."

Santonio chuckled, shaking his head. "Munchies. If yo ass would go down there and cook, a nigga wouldn't be starving."

"I told you I'm not cooking two dinners in one day, Santonio." I gave him the side-eye. We ate dinner at nine. It was now going on twelve-thirty.

"I'm waiting." He put the bowl to his lips, so he could drink the milk.

"You can love people and not give them the opportunity to hurt you."

"Mmmm." He nodded, wiping his mouth down. "Who said that?"

"Me."

"So that's a note?"

I sighed. "Yeah."

"How you come to that conclusion?" Santonio turned sideways to look at me. "Why you feel like that? It's kind of like, 'loving people from a distance,' right?"

"I guess you could say that. The only thing is, when you love a person from a distance, a disconnect forms." I stared down at the page. "We can't control what people do or say, but we can control how we react, right?"

"Right." Santonio stared at me.

"I was so busy trying to fix everybody else's problems, I ignored my own." I started scribbling around the word *perception*. "I was talking to Skyy when we were in Arizona and she told me to stop crying over spilled milk." I traced the letters.

Even though I'd heard that statement a hundred times, her saying it during our conversation made something in my brain click. I was making my life harder than it needed to be. Lately, I'd been stressing over shit that I had no control over. People were going to be people, and most people I knew were hurting. I had to accept that I didn't have all the answers and I made mistakes because I was imperfect.

I was sure I'd made plenty of fucked up decisions that affected other people. I couldn't change my past, but I could definitely make adjustments in my present, and stay optimistic about my future. I was willing to accept and take ownership for my faults in any relationship I felt was failing or had failed. And I was starting with my family. My mom, then Eli, and lastly, my grandmother.

"It's crazy cause I'm learning myself through you." He sat the bowl down on the floor.

"How?" I asked with a raised eyebrow. If anybody was the student, it was me.

"When I first met you, you had an attitude."

I laughed. "No I didn't."

"Lil nigga, please. You was high as fuck too."

"Yep." I smiled. "That was the first time Skyy introduced me to Deidra. And you were outside in the car."

He nodded. "I was just scoping the scene." Santonio looked up at the ceiling. "Looked back into my review... and got stuck. So, you know I had to get out and mack you down."

I smacked my lips. "Yeah, okay. You got my number from Skyy and begged to cook for me. Desperate ass." I snickered.

"I just wanted to be around you. Your energy was different, even with that mean mug."

I rolled my eyes.

"After you had Toni, I started to see that mean mug and that attitude for what it was."

I titled my head in wonderment. We stared directly in each other's eyes as I waited for him to elaborate.

"Sadness." His tongue swiped his bottom lip, eyebrow dipped in frustration. "You wasn't mad at the world, you was sad at what the world had done to you. And shit, in my honest opinion, a hurt person does more long-term damage than an angry person does."

I looked down, grabbed my pen, and quickly jotted that down.

"When I met you, you was holding on to hurt. Not just from that bitch ass nigga, TreVell, but the shit wit' ya fam too. Then you was arguing every other day wit' ya homegirls. You was fighting bitches cause I was fuckin' off. You got pregnant and then Jeanette got smoked."

As I listened to him run down my last four and a half years, my eyebrows furrowed.

"See." With a blank expression, his eyes danced around me. "You not even mad. I hurt your feelings."

I broke our gaze and looked at the TV mounted on the wall. "So how are you learning yourself through me?" I smirked sarcastically, still staring at the TV displaying "State Property." Santonio was supposed to be watching it since he picked it, but he hadn't sat down and looked at it once. "What? You sad too?" I scoffed.

Five seconds passed and he didn't respond, so I faced him. The look in his eyes slowed my breathing. I must've been giving him a funny look because he looked away and ran his palm across his waves. I tossed the journal next to me and crawled towards him. He gave me a side smile as he pulled me into his lap.

"I'm proud of you, E." He caressed my collar bone. "You came a long way, baby."

I laid my head on his shoulder. "Whenever you're feeling sad, you can talk to me."

He nodded. "I know. You the only person I trust wit' my secrets. That's why I'm making you wife."

I smiled. "Aw, baby, that's sweet." I pulled gently at his beard.

"Just speakin' facts." Santonio kissed my forehead. We sat there quietly with his head resting on top of mine.

A sudden calmness came down on me. I got teary eyed as we listened to each other breathe. I read somewhere that you should grow by one percent every day. And that's exactly what Santonio was doing. He was opening up to me, showing vulnerability.

Santonio's heart was big, which was why he loved so hard. He only acted unruly to mask his pain. It was crazy how I could see that in him before I saw it in myself. We'd grown together, bounced knowledge off one another without even realizing it.

Santonio's phone went off and he reached into his pocket. Xenia's name flashed across the screen and I crossed my arms. "Why is she calling so late?"

He ignored me, answered the phone and put it to his ear. "Wassup?"

I frowned.

"Nah."

My eyes swept to the television and then back to him.

"That could've waited until tomorrow." His irritation was evident. "Because ain't shit I can do about it right now."

I got out of his lap, grabbed the bowl, and left the room. As I made my way through our home, I still couldn't believe it was actually mine. After washing the bowl and spoon, I put them in the dish rack and started back upstairs.

When I entered the room, I didn't see Santonio, but I heard shower water running. I climbed back into bed and just as I picked up my journal, his phone went off. My eyes shot toward the bathroom door and then back to the phone lying face up. I crawled across the bed and snatched it up. Xenia's name flashed across the screen.

"Hello," I answered.

"Can you put Santonio on the phone?"

"He's busy. He'll call you tomorrow." If whatever she had to say was so important, she would've told him during their last conversation.

"I didn't know he a personal assistant. I'll just leave a message with you and you can deliver it to him." She chuckled.

"Girl, fuck you." I hung up the phone and threw his phone down. I then stared at the bathroom door.

*I was just saying we were going in the right direction and he goes and pulls this shit!*

I bit down on my bottom lip as I continued glaring at the door. I counted back from five and then looked down at my engagement ring. I stared off in thought as I twisted it a few times. After I grabbed my journal, and a pen, I flipped to a blank page. I didn't want to jump to conclusions, but I was still dealing with insecurities from being cheated on.

Why was Xenia calling so much and so late? Santonio admitted she wanted to fuck, and his extensive rap sheet didn't help his case. How could he work closely with someone who was attracted to him and obviously didn't care he had a woman? I looked back down at the blank page and tapped the pen on the page. I glanced once more at the door and then back down.

*"Love can make me cry, laugh, yell, sing and doubt myself all in one day. It makes me cynical and sometimes I feel like I'm compromising my sanity. But those are the lows. The highs are like first time you fly in plane and see the clouds right outside your window."*

# TONE

I was sliding my third and last chain over my head when I realized Erin hadn't spoke to me since I got out the shower. I fastened my watch and grabbed a coat from a hanger. Our closet looked like department store. Mirrors, jewelry shelves, shoe racks and clothing took up a lot of space but there was still a lot of room to move around. Before I made my way out, I grabbed a Toronto Raptors fitted. I slipped it over my head as I stepped out of the closet.

"What's wrong wit' you?" I stopped by the dresser and grabbed my burner. I tucked it into my jeans and approached the bed.

"Nothing," she mumbled.

"It's something." I sat down on the bed to fix the bottom of my pants. I then retied the shoestrings to my black Timbs. "Spit it out."

I knew she wasn't mad about me leaving late. I had some shit to take care of. Erin wasn't new to this. I had been home all day. I wasn't even gon' be gone that long. If I left now, then I would be back before four thirty.

"Did you fuck Xenia when you went to Portland?"

I frowned. "You trippin' cause she called? I'ma handle it." Xenia was gon' make me kick her ass. She was causing chaos in my fortress of peace.

"She called back."

"Okay." I stood up.

"Did you fuck her in Portland?"

"No."

Erin cut her eyes at me like she didn't believe me.

"You trippin'." I shook my head. I grabbed a phone off the bed and two more off my dresser. "I told you what it was."

"Just get the fuck out. I'm not even bout to waste my time," she spat, sliding her ring off. She started to storm pass me and I snatched her up.

"Put your fuckin' ring back on."

She mugged me. "No."

"What the fuck you want me to do? Not make money? Disrespect the Dons?"

"I want you to let me go." She sighed.

"I didn't fuck her, and I don't plan to. Shorty is messy, and I'm handle that. A'ight?" I made her look at me. "Now put your ring on."

When she pushed away from me, I let her go and she headed for the bathroom.

"I love you. If you up when I'm on my way home, I'll bring you some Town Topic," I called over my shoulder as I left the room.

"Dio, I'm guessing your assistant delivered my message."

"Xenia, this desperate shit you on gon' get you murked, shorty." I pulled into the parking lot of True's bar.

"Did you just threaten me?"

"You heard me." I found a spot and put my whip in park. "I can't do business with a muthafucka that's putting stress on my home life."

When Xenia showed up to my room in nothing but a trench coat, I'd looked her over slowly, painted a mental picture and shut the door in her face. I took a cold shower and then call Erin and had her play with her pussy while I listened. I hadn't never done no shit like that; that was how I knew I wanted E to be my wife. Xenia called me twenty times and sent text messages talking shit. She thought I was playing with her, so I was about to make some shit clear.

"Bitch, I don't care who your daddy is. You hear me, Xenia? Just like you got a army of men, I got one too and we go to war wit' whoever, shorty. Stop fuckin' tryin' me."

"You know, Santonio, I should've known you were weak." Xenia's voice went up an octave. "You'd rather chase love instead of making millions. It's pathetic."

"Don't call my phone no more on bullshit." I hung up and called Erin. She didn't answer the first time, so I called her right back.

"Hello?"

"I ain't gon' be gone that long, so stay yo ass up. I'ma fix that attitude."

She smacked her lips. "Is that why you called me? Santonio, why are you trying to make me mad?"

"Cause you cute when you poutin.'" I watched three cars pull into the parking lot.

"Whatever, we were getting along just fine before that Xenia bitch called. You handled that, right?"

"Yeah."

"Santonio, if she keeps on, that means you're allowing her." She sighed. "Which means I'ma assume you're fuckin' her and then I'ma stop fuckin' wit' you."

"It's like that?" I chuckled.

"Straight like that."

I opened my door, turned sideways, and placed my feet on the concrete. "I hear you, boss." I dapped up Ro and Drake. "What you want from Town Topic?"

"Breakfast sandwich and some hash browns."

"A'ight. Is that ring on?"

She snickered.

"I'm not laughing." I FaceTimed her and she answered wearing a pink bonnet. "Let me see."

Erin held her hand up.

"A'ight. I'll see you in a minute. I love you."

"I love you too."

"E got that ass trained already, I see." Roman chuckled as soon as I hung up.

I ignored him, got out the car, and shut the door. "Where True at?"

"He already here." We made our way to the entrance.

"Chance dropped him off. They had they lil' best friend day today." Roman shook his head.

When we got inside, I sat at the bar, Ro went to look for a remote to turn one of the TVs on, and Drake headed for True's office. After the New Year, me and Ro were going to Minnesota. That was in three days. I planned on spending a couple days there. I figured that would give me enough time to convince Rome to move to Kansas City and to take care of some other business. I had to make sure shit here was straight when we left, and since Que was in Texas, that left Drake and True.

I trusted them to keep the streets on lock in our absence. Lil' niggas respected True cause he still kicked it in the slums every day. True moved like he didn't have a bunch of money; he wasn't flashy, and he didn't boast. Drake just got out of the jam, and just like True, he was a bully. Even with him being locked up for eight years, his name rang in the streets.

The TVs above the bar cut on. "I'm tired as fuck." Roman flipped through the channels.

"Ava usually have yo ass in the bed by eight, that's why." True approached the bar grinning. "Wassup, Tone." We slapped fives.

"'Sup."

He went behind the bar. "What y'all niggas got up?"

"Shit." Ro took a seat.

I watched as True sat an Ace of Spades bottle and four double shot glasses on the counter. "Ro was telling me y'all shootin' out to Minneapolis after the new year."

I grabbed a shot and tossed it back. "Yeah, we need to take care of this Rome situation."

True was like family. He and Roman had been tight since they were young. Roman vouched for him which was enough for me. I didn't know what to expect from Rome once I met her, but I needed to be focused on that without stressing about the home front. True would look out for my family like they were his and he was about his paper, so he wasn't easily distracted. I knew True would hold it down.

Drake emerged from the back eating a sandwich.

"This nigga always eatin'." True chuckled.

"I need for you and Drake to be my eyes and ears for a couple days."

True nodded.

"Where y'all niggas goin'?" he asked before taking a big bite.

"Minnesota." I stared at him. "I don't need for you to be on no hot shit." He had spent the last eight years of his life locked up, three of those he spent in solitary confinement. Drake was a dark nigga, so sometimes he just lashed out. Deidra dying made him worse.

He scoffed, still eating.

"Drake, you just got home. Keep the heat off of you for a little while, nigga." Drake was making up for missed time by partying, blowing money, and fuckin' bitches. He was a disrespectful ass nigga too, so he already had a lot of unnecessary beef.

He tossed his chin up.

"If niggas start testin' you, just lay 'em down. Don't even do the back and forth. But don't be messy with the shit." I looked back and forth between him and True. On top of Deidra dying, I had been moving around a lot lately and I was sure niggas noticed. I didn't want them to get too comfortable; they still had to answer to me.

True tossed his shot back. "Say less."

# 17

# CHANGES

ERIN

"Moms." I called out to Sadee as I let myself in her home. She hadn't been answering the phone, so I got worried and drove down the road.

I shut the door behind me and started through the foyer. Her house was quiet, and it didn't smell like she'd cooked anything which was unusual for Sadee. She was always either baking, cooking, or putting puzzles together. I made my way through the first level and when I didn't come across her, I headed for the stairs. As I climbed them, I heard what sounded like a soft moan.

I stopped in my tracks. I had to be tripping. The moaning got louder, and I covered my hand with my mouth when I heard Ms. Sadee cry out to someone named Grey. I turned around and quietly descended the steps. There was only one Grey I knew and that was her driver.

I hurriedly made my exit and before I could shut her front door all the way, I burst out laughing. I laughed so hard my insides felt like they were being twisted. Tears rolled down my cheeks and my breaths got short. I had to take a seat on the small step just to pull myself together. I couldn't believe Sadee was getting it in with Grey.

I wasn't mad at her. Grey was GQ handsome. He always wore tailored suits with shiny expensive shoes. His salt and peppered Caesar, beard, and mustache were always well kept, and he was a complete gentleman. I laughed again. Ms. Sadee had bagged her a young tenderoni.

After a minute or two passed, I stood up, shaking my head. I headed back to my car with a wide grin on my face.

"Gon' head, Ms. Sadee."

AFTER I LEFT SADEE'S, I went back home and got the girls dressed nice and snug for the weather. Santonio had built a whole playground for the girls in the backyard. It was equipped with a slide, swings, a little merry-go-round, monkey bars, spring riders and a club house. When he first had it built, I told him he was doing too much. Now, I appreciated the amenity. Sanaa played on her jungle gym as I held Toni by her arms, egging her on to take steps. Her little legs bucked lightly as she babbled loud.

"Mommy, look!" Sanaa shouted.

I looked up just in time so see her sliding down the slide.

"Clap for your sister, Toni." I laughed, helping her. "Say yay, Sanaa."

Toni babbled.

"Ayo, E."

I looked back towards the house and Royal was standing with my mother. She had a frustrated look on her face as she trekked in my direction. I picked Toni up and noticed Royal hadn't moved.

"She's good, Royal."

"A'ight." He nodded before going back inside.

"What the fuck was that about?" My mom frowned. "I kept telling him I was your mother. He even called you. Where is your phone?"

"In the house." I had forgotten it in Toni's room after I changed her diaper. I wasn't in a rush to get to it either. Santonio went out of town to get Rome, and my girls were with me. Tone said he probably wouldn't be able to talk until later on tonight, and I was busy with my babies. I didn't have a need for my cellphone, so I wasn't pressed for it.

"Why is the compound on lockdown like Fort Knox? What the hell is going on?" She held her arms out for Toni, but she laid her head on my chest. "You don't want to come to Grandma, Toni?"

"Santonio says we have to have security." I tried to pry Toni off of me, but she wasn't having it. "He doesn't want to take any chances."

"Hi, Grandma!" Sanaa ran up and jumped into her arms.

"Hi, baby. Ya mama got you out here in the cold?" My mom picked Sanaa up, kissed her cheek, and then put her back down.

Sanaa took back off towards the jungle gym.

"If it's that serious, then you don't need to be here."

"What?" I put Toni down back down on her feet. I held her arms as she bounced around.

"If he has to do all this just to keep you safe, then you need to think about what's best for your daughters and you."

I rolled my eyes.

"You wanna live like this, Erin? Having to pay strangers to watch over your back?" My mom shook her head in disapproval.

I chuckled. "Let me get this straight. It's okay for Santonio to make his money illegally, he's just not supposed to have too much?" Was she absent-minded? Eli wasn't a saint. She wasn't even working but had a house paid off in her name and was pushing a brand new Tesla. Not to mention she was always shopping and recently she had caught the traveling bug.

"You know that's not what I mean." Her nose scrunched up. "Eli knows limits, Tone doesn't. He's power hungry, and that's gon' be his downfall, watch."

I stared down at Toni.

"Then you're going to marry him?"

"Yeah, Mama, I am." I picked Toni up. "I wanna marry him."

"Why? Because he buys you nice things? Erin, at what cost? You have two daughters to protect. No amount of security will keep them safe if Tone makes the wrong enemy."

I sat down on the bench. "Ma, I'm marrying him. I love him, and I wanna continue to build with him. I have faith that Tone will do anything to protect us. Which is why you could barely get in the house." I looked up at her. "'Cause I can guarantee since Royal has never met you, he searched you."

She scowled. "You think that shit is cute?"

"No, but it keeps us safe," I shot back. She had me fucked up if she thought she was coming over here to change my mind or turn me against Santonio. She was telling me shit I already knew. Things I had already prayed and meditated about.

"Wow." My mom shook her head as disappointment burned in her gaze. "You're settling, Erin."

"Then let me learn from my mistakes, Ma." I pleaded with my eyes for her support my decision. "You had to bump your head a few times too and I'm not holding that against you. That's life. You live, and you learn." I glanced over at Sanaa who was trying to sit her American Girl doll straight up on the swing.

"I just don't want you to get your hopes up and he disappoints you again, Erin." She crossed her arms. "Marriage is a huge step."

"I know."

"And you want to take that step with him?"

"Yeah, I do." I stared at her. "So, I would appreciate if you just backed me up. You're allowed to feel the way you do. But you're wasting your energy being mad about something you can't change or control."

My mom looked up at the sky and groaned lightly. She looked back down at me and dropped down next to me on the bench. "Why are you so hard headed?"

I chuckled.

"You really love that lil' nappy headed boy?"

I adjusted Toni's gloves. "I do."

"What if he doesn't change?" I could see her staring at me through my peripheral vision.

I looked over at her and for the first time, instead of disapproval, I saw concern. I understood where her anxiety was stemming from, but it was a new year. A new day, with new battles. I couldn't keep living in what used to be, or what could've been. I had to live in the "right now."

"What if he does?"

# TONE

"This is it." Roman pulled up in front a beat down, dirty, dingy looking building. Just like the other buildings surrounding it, it looked like it was 'bout to fall over any second.

I checked my surroundings and quickly noticed there were only a few people outside. A few kids were playing around in the courtyard and some young cats were shooting dice further down the sidewalk.

"She living in the projects and shit." Roman clenched his jaw. "Her ass is coming home, today."

"Chill out." I looked at the side mirror. "You can't be goin' in here demanding shit like you know her. Anybody could be up in there." I opened the passenger door and got out.

"Fuck all that." Roman pulled his hoody over his head. "She ain't got no choice."

The sidewalks were cracked badly, and the grass was filled with trash. I noticed a majority of the windows were either broken or had blinds that were falling apart. It smelled like sewage too; like a bunch of backed up drains. I looked over my shoulder once more before we started climbing a set of raggedy, wooden steps. They were creaking badly and damn near wobbling.

When we reached apartment 3107, Roman knocked on the door

and stepped back. We waited a few seconds and then he knocked again. I checked the time on my watch and seen it was a little after one in the evening. I had been having her followed for a couple days, and she was usually home around this time. Roman knocked again.

Even though Ava had located Rome, we hadn't been able to get in touch with her. Her ass didn't answer the phone for unknown numbers, listen to voicemails, or read her emails. She didn't even know we were coming, so I already knew this visit could only go one of two ways.

"Who are you looking for?"

I turned around and my eyes landed on a young woman. Her hair was braided in black plaits that hung down to her waist. Her dark brown eyes bounced back and forth between me and Roman in curiosity. Her perfectly arched eyebrows furrowed and then she crossed her arms. My eyes then roamed her body and I frowned at the tight ass acid wash jeans she was wearing.

"You Rome?" Roman asked after he assessed her. I was sure he noticed how much she favored him.

"Why?" She looked at me. "Do I know you?"

"Nah..." I shook my head. "Can we go inside? Or you can ride out with us to go get something to eat." I gave her two options and waited for her to answer.

"Uh, I don't know either one of you. I'm not letting you inside and I'm definitely not going anywhere with you." She reached into her pea coat and removed a switch blade.

"The fuck you gon' do with that?" Roman chuckled.

Rome's head snapped in his direction. "I will cut you the fuck up out here. Try me." She sneered.

I held my hands up. "All that ain't even called for, shorty."

"What is this? You some kind of perverts?" Rome frowned. "Did you follow me home from the club?"

Yeah, my little sister was a bottle girl at strip joint. When the private detective told me, at first, I didn't think nothing of it. I cringed when he told me she was walking around the club topless. When he tried to show me the pictures, I tossed them muthafuckas in the fireplace.

"We yo brothers," Roman blurted. "And it's cold as fuck out here. Open the door."

Rome's right eyebrow rose, and her eyes darkened. "I don't have brothers. Sisters either. You have the wrong person." She adjusted the glasses on her face. "Now can you please get from in front of my door?"

"You Rome Morris, right?" I asked, and she stared at me. "I'm Santonio Morris, and this Roman Morris." Even though she was acting tough swinging a blade around, I could see how tense she was. She was afraid. "We all have the same pops," I pointed at Roman. "You and him have the same mama."

Rome's eyes rolled to Roman. She looked him over slowly and I was guessing she saw some similarities because her face softened. "You were put up for adoption too?"

"Can you let us in? We'll answer any question you have," I assured her.

She stalled for a minute and then removed her keys from her coat pocket. She unlocked her door, stepped inside, and then ushered for us to come inside. As soon as I entered, I noticed it smelled like Gain dryer sheets. Roman shut the door and Rome ventured to the end table by the window and turned the lamp on. She then removed her coat and tossed it over the arm of the loveseat.

Rome's apartment was nice and clean. It was nothing like the outside. Everything was either black, white, or grey. The wooden floors were shiny, and since the little apartment had an open floor plan, I was able to see her kitchen was spotless. Rome headed for the back of her apartment without a word.

I took a seat on the couch and Roman stood in front of the door. A few minutes passed before she returned and when she did, she was carrying a little white dog wearing pink bows, and a shiny collar. She had dressed down in a pair of black sweats and a white T and had taken off her heels and was now wearing a pair of black socks. She even pulled the front of her hair up in bun.

Rome was pretty. I could definitely see the family resemblance. She had a piercing right above her top lip in the middle, and both of her ears were lined from the top to the bottom with diamond studs. She had a few tattoos on her arms, and a big red rose on the front of her neck. She reached under the couch, grabbed a Nike shoe box, and then plopped down on the couch next to me.

"Y'all smoke?"

I shook my head.

"You can sit down, twin." She glanced at Roman and smirked. "I promise ain't nobody coming through. My dick appointment just fell through." She removed a sack and a pack of shells out of the box.

I frowned.

Roman sucked his teeth. "Don't nobody wanna hear that shit." He took a seat on the loveseat.

Rome snickered. "Can you toss me that remote?" She started breaking weed down on the box. "Or just press the power button." She reached into her sweats for her phone.

Roman did what she asked.

"Alexa," she called out. "Play DaniLeigh, 'The Plan.'"

Once the music started playing, she turned the volume down a little using her phone.

"So, how did you find me?" She concentrated on breaking down the weed.

Roman leaned back into his seat. "We just found out about you from our triflin' ass mama."

Rome nodded. "So...you know Macie?" she asked, now splitting a grape swisher down the middle.

I tilted my head. "You knew who ya moms was? Why didn't you reach out?"

She shrugged. "Why bother someone who don't wanna be bothered?" She bobbed her head coolly to the music.

"She ain't your only family. Everybody stays in Kansas City, Missouri," I told her.

"Our daddy too?" Rome dumped the guts out of the blunt into a plastic bag. All while swaying her head from side to side, mouthing the words to the song.

"Nah, that nigga dead."

She nodded.

"So how old are you?" she started, sealing the blunt closed.

"Thirty. I'ma be thirty-one this year."

Her gaze landed on Roman. "And you?"

"Twenty-eight."

"Guess that makes me the baby." Rome smirked. "Is that why you came here? Cause I'm not a baby. I'll be twenty in April." She grabbed a lighter. "The second. Just throwing that out there in case y'all give gifts."

I smirked.

Roman leaned forward. "You comin' wit' us."

"Am I?" Rome put the blunt to her lips and sparked it. She took a long toke, inhaled, held it in, and then blew smoke from her nostrils. "Says who?" She stared at Roman.

"Your big bros."

"I don't know y'all, and I don't have enough bread saved up to just be moving out of state." She tried to pass the weed to me and I shook my head again. "I can visit for a few days. I don't do shit else if I'm not working." She tried to hand the blunt to Roman and he mugged her.

"Money ain't a issue."

Rome looked back and forth between me and Ro. "What y'all do for a living? That G-Wagon in the front yours?"

I nodded.

"You a drug dealer?"

"I'm a businessman."

"You too?" she asked Roman.

He shrugged.

We sat quietly as Rome smoked her blunt and vibed to her music. I could tell she was in her head. She had a lot to consider on such short notice. At first, my plan was to let her make the decision, but after seeing her living conditions, she didn't have a say.

Rome's little dog sat protectively in front of the door, biting on a toy. She looked like a tiny teddy bear, not a guard dog. Nothing was threatening about her little ass.

When Rome got down to the last of her blunt, she grabbed the Nike box again. "I'll go, but I wanna make my own money." She stared at me. "Put me on."

I glanced at Roman, who was already looking at me with a frown on his face.

# 18

# LET IT ALL WORK OUT...

ERIN

I pushed the front door open, and Sanaa took off running down the hall. "Walk Naa!" I called after her, shutting the door with my butt. I knew she was going to find her daddy. She knew he was home because his car was parked in the front.

I made my way to the family room with a sleeping Toni in my arms. We had just gotten out of church and parted with Sadee. She was cooking dinner and I agreed to help after I changed my clothes. She still didn't know I had heard her and Grey, and I didn't plan on speaking on it no time soon. I sat down on the couch and started removing Toni's coat.

She stirred a little in her sleep before sticking her middle and index fingers in her mouth.

I gently tried to take her fingers out, but she started whining. "We not gon' start that habit." I kissed her cheek.

After putting her in her swing, I removed my coat and went to hang it up.

"I don't have to answer to you, that's why." I heard an unfamiliar voice down the hall.

I hung my coat up and closed the closet door.

"Do what you gotta do then. I'm not going to argue with you."

I poked my head in the family room to make sure Toni was still sleep. After I was sure she was good, I followed the voice.

"I'ma just change my number."

I entered the kitchen and a chick wearing jeans and a Tommy Hilfiger cut off windbreaker was standing in front of the microwave. She tilted her head, flipped her long box braids to the side and smacked her lips. "Bye, nigga." She then dropped the phone on the counter and started humming a soft melody.

"You Rome?" I asked, taking a seat at the island.

She spun around, looked me over and smiled. "Yeah. Erin?"

I nodded.

Rome was gorgeous. One look at her and you knew she was a Chauhan. Whoever their daddy was had some strong genes. They all had that button nose and slanted eyes, and thick eyelashes. I could see underneath those braids she had soft, silky hair like Roman. Santonio's hair was the same texture but he kept his in a fade. The only thing that separated her from them was her milk chocolate complexion. She'd gotten that from Macie.

She crossed her arms. "Nice to meet you."

"You too."

"Tonio and Twin told me a little about their women." Rome switched back to the microwave and removed a bag of popcorn. "Did he tell you I'm staying here?"

"We talked about it." I figured she would. I just didn't know what to expect. Erica was already moving in and now Rome. That made the total four. Four women in my home under the age of twenty-one.

*This should be fun.*

"Twin thinks I have a bad attitude." She shrugged and poured popcorn into a big, plastic bowl. Twin was the perfect nickname for Roman, they looked so much alike. "So he said I can't stay with him. He said Ava was enough."

I chuckled.

Rome snickered as she threw the popcorn bag away. When she

faced me again, I instantly recognized she was high as hell. Her eyes weren't red, but they were glossy and low. "I told him to tell Ava I don't want no problems." She walked to my side of the island and sat two chairs down. "Want some?"

I shook my head.

We sat quietly as I checked my text messages and Rome chomped down on popcorn. She sighed a couple times and then she turned sideways in her seat and faced me.

"I think I made a huge mistake coming here."

I looked at her. "You tell Santonio that?"

Rome shrugged. "I don't think it would've mattered." She glanced at the entryway. "Tonio doesn't scare you? I mean, I've seen some scary niggas in my lifetime, but he's...frightening." She said that with a straight face and then burst into a fit of laughter. "He's so damn serious and Twin is rude as fuck." She shook her head. "I didn't even wanna chance it." Rome laughed some more at her own expense and then grabbed a handful of popcorn. "Plus, this is better than living in the hood. My lights were about to get cut off."

I heard the pitter patter of little feet and then Sanaa rounded the corner slowly carrying the smallest puppy I'd ever seen. She was cute with her big brown eyes, pink bows, and glitter collar. Sanaa walked her to me and held her up for me to take her. I took the puppy and held her up over my head to examine her. She smelled good and she was too damn cute. She looked like a fluffy piece of cotton.

"Awww," I cooed.

"Her name is Grizzy B." Rome handed Sanaa some popcorn.

"Grizzy B?" I laughed. The lil' puppy didn't not look like a "Grizzy B." Rome had to be playing. When her facial expression didn't change, I shook my head. "Why would you name her Grizzy B?" I chuckled. "Say I'm too cute for that name..." I baby-talked to Grizzy B.

Sanaa thought that was funny. Her little giggle made Rome laugh.

"Her full name is Griselda Blanco."

I smacked my lips. "Why would you name your dog after the

'Queen of Cocaine'?" I was learning quickly that Rome's ass was goofy.

"Don't sleep on my girl." Rome laughed. "And it fits perfectly. She's white like coke, and she's fluffy like a Grizzly bear. 'Grizzy B.'"

*She must've been high when she came up with that.*

"Grizzy B, why yo mama do you like that?" I cooed, getting more giggles out of Sanaa. I sat her down on the floor and she took off running out of the living room.

"She's fully housetrained." Rome handed Sanaa the bowl and then stood up. "When I go to sleep, she gets in her own bed, and if I leave the house she comes with me, or I put her in her cage before I bounce."

I nodded. "We're going to your aunt's house in a minute if you wanna come. She cooks Sunday dinner after church every week now that she lives right down the road."

Rome dried her hands off on a paper towel. "Sadee. Tonio's mom, right?"

"Yep."

"What if she doesn't like me?" Rome tossed the towel into the trash bin. "I mean, Macie *did* run off with her man."

"Sadee's not like that. She's going to love you regardless because you're blood." Plus, I'd already had a heart to heart with Sadee. She explained everything that went down with their daddy and her. He was abusive, but he provided. That was why she stayed with him. After she had Santonio, he distanced himself from her and then started an affair with Macie. When Macie got pregnant, he didn't want the baby and convinced her to leave Roman with Sadee. Sadee sadly admitted she didn't stop doing drugs until after she took Roman in.

Rome shrugged. "I'll go. But I wouldn't even be mad at her if she didn't wanna fuck with me."

"Awww..." Sanaa looked up at her.

"Mess..." Rome snickered. "If she doesn't *mess* with me." She grabbed her phone.

I hopped down of my seat and started out of the kitchen. "Okay, we'll leave in about twenty." I called over my shoulder.

"My niece is cuter than yours..." I heard Rome. "Nani-poo say 'wassup Snap.'"

I chuckled at Sanaa doing what she said as I went to go look for Santonio.

# TONE

When Erin entered our bedroom, I was on the phone wrapping up a conversation with Don Capporelli. I watched her switch towards me and then looked up at her when she stood in between my legs. She twisted her engagement ring as she waited on me to get off the phone.

"I expect to see you there." He mumbled. "Take care, Santonio." He hung up.

I tossed my phone onto the bed and grabbed two handfuls of Erin's ass. "What you want?"

She smacked her lips. "Hi to you too." I pulled her onto my lap and she straddled me. "I haven't seen you in almost three days."

I kissed her neck. "What you do today?"

Erin wrapped her arms around my neck. "Went to church. I'm about to go help your mom cook. She wants everything do be done by five."

I frowned. "I'm hungry now."

"We had a big breakfast."

I looked at my watch. "It's almost twelve thirty. You need to be leaving then."

"Really?" She laughed. "You don't wanna kiss on me a little?" She pouted playfully.

My burner phone sounded off.

"Rome seems cool." Erin tugged at my beard. "She's really pretty and Sanaa's up under her already."

I massaged her thighs. "She a'ight. I still need to get to know her." I noticed Rome smoked a lot. She'd smoked three blunts already and she had only been up since nine. She didn't really eat either. If she did, she was snacking on chips and shit.

"She's silly. You know she named her dog after Griselda Blanco?" E laughed. "That's definitely your little sister." She chuckled.

"I was going to put her up in an apartment, but I want her on the compound." Nobody knew she was my sister yet, but I couldn't risk her safety in case somebody found out.

"I know."

"The other house too big for just her." I lay back. "I was gon' give it to her and Erica, but I can already see me killing one of these little niggas."

Erin frowned. "That's too much house for them, anyway. She's cool here." She then crawled up my body and looked down directly in my face. "That's five ladies in one house." She smiled. "You ready for that?"

I pulled her shirt over her head. "Just remember you promised me a boy."

I knew Ma Duke was nervous about meeting Rome. She kept texting me, asking me about her, and what kind of foods she liked. Just like us, she didn't know what to expect. The good thing about that was Rome was nothing like *I* expected. When the private investigator told me she worked in a strip club, I prepared for a loud mouth, shiesty, angry bitch that was mad at the world. Rome was nothing like that. She was quiet for the most part, and she laughed a lot.

We had just pulled up to Ma Duke's spot. Rome didn't even look up from her phone or take her headphones off. She sighed a few times and then started texting. I pulled her ear plug out.

"You ready?"

"I think I'ma just meet her tomorrow. I'm tired." Her phone still held her attention. "My stomach is hurting. I think I'm bout to start my period."

I scowled at her. "Don't nobody wanna hear all that, man."

She shrugged.

"Get out." I opened my door and got out. When she didn't move, I shut my door and ventured to the passenger side. I pulled the door and motioned for her to come on. "Let's go."

"Tonio, I don't feel good." She rested back comfortably in her seat.

"I don't give a fuck." Wasn't shit wrong with her ass, she was just nervous.

Rome stared at me defiantly. "You don't control me."

"Santonio, who do we have here?" Ma Duke saved her just as I was about to snatch her stubborn ass out of the truck.

I stepped back. "Ma, this Rome. She was just telling me she don't wanna meet your old ass."

Rome's eyes widened in disbelief and Ma Duke hit my arm. "Watch your mouth, boy."

I pointed at Rome. "I didn't say it, she did."

"No, I did not!" Rome shrieked. "How you gon' stand there and lie like that?"

Ma Duke chuckled. "Don't pay him any mind, honey." She smiled at Rome. "Hop out and let me look at you."

I frowned when Rome wasted no time getting out. "Ain't that some shit. Her hard-headed ass can stay here with you then."

"You're gorgeous." Ma Duke ignored me and pulled her into a hug. "You look so much like your father." She stared at her for a while. "I'm Sadee."

"Rome." They shared an embrace. "Tonio and Twin told me so much you." Rome looked back at moms. Her eyes usually stayed glossy or red since she smoked so much, but the moisture that lingered in them at that moment tugged at my heart strings.

Ma Duke pulled her into another hug. "You hungry? You like yams and greens? Cornbread? What's your favorite kind of cake? I stopped and got a honey baked ham. I wasn't sure if you ate ham, so I fried chicken too, regular and buffalo." Ma Duke rambled off and then she wrapped her arm into Rome's. "Roman will be here later, but his girlfriend and son are here." They headed for the house. "Your aunties, uncles, and cousins want to meet you too. They should be dropping by later."

"So, you're kicking me out?" Rome turned to look at me. She sounded tough, but those eyes told a different story.

"Of course, he's not." Ma Duke said sternly. "Don't listen to him."

Rome smacked her lips. "I won't stay somewhere I'm not wanted." She crossed her arms and walked into the house behind Ma Duke as I held the door open for them.

"Shut up." I was just about to shut the door when Aunt Paige's car pulled up. The passenger door swung open and Macie hopped out.

"Sadee!" she screamed, rushing towards the house.

"Y'all ain't right!" Aunt Paige yelled.

Rome stopped in her tracks and headed back for the door. Ma Duke kept on walking.

"Man, don't bring that shit to my mama's house." At the hospital, I had learned Ma Duke had high blood pressure, and she suffered from insomnia. I couldn't have these nobodies getting her all worked up.

Rome stood next to me to quietly.

Macie started crying and Paige continued cursing. "Tone, you know this is fucked up. When Rome got here, the first person you should've brought her to see is her mama! Sadee's ass knows she wrong too. That's why she won't come out here!"

"Nah." Ava pushed past me. "She won't come out here because I told her I would handle her, lightweight, bitch!" She started to take off just as Erin grabbed her and held her back.

"You gon' let these bitches jump on your family?!" Paige screamed. "Nigga, I will call my son. Best believe he'll gladly go back to jail for his mama."

"What type of dumb shit is that?!" Ava yelled. "E, let me go. I'm 'bout to drag this bitch by that old ass wig!"

"Go ahead and try me! I got nieces that will dog you out, little girl." Paige wouldn't let up. She rushed back to the car. "Watch this!"

"Rome..." Macie cried. "I want to talk to you."

Rome's eyebrows damn near touched as she looked back at her mother.

"Don't let them turn you against me."

"No, this deadbeat didn't." Ava chuckled. "E, just let me her smack one time."

Rome didn't say a word, just stood there and stared blankly at Macie.

"I know I made some decisions that I regret, but baby, I never stopped thinking about you." She sniffled. "You and your brother are all I have left."

Rome spun around and walked into the house.

"Macie, take yo ass on, man. If Rome wanna holler at you, I'll swing by that way later on." I looked down at Erin and Ava. "Go in the house."

Ava took of first. Erin started behind her and I followed her into the house. "Is Paige calling your cousins over here?"

"Paige is trippin'." My cousins knew what was up. I was helping damn near all of them out with *something*. Not mention that they all loved my mother too much to even feed into that bullshit. There were plenty of times when Ma Duke fed them as kids or made sure they had clean clothes or somewhere safe to sleep at night. Paige and Macie were just mad that Rome had chosen Ma Duke. Her sisters couldn't handle what we all did.

# 19

# ALL I WANT IS YOU

ERIN

I cut the car off and then stared out of the window. It was sprinkling a little, but for some strange reason, the sun was out. Here it was coming towards the third week of January, but it wasn't that chilly. Headstones were lined perfectly along the manicured grass. I took a deep breath and coached myself silently. The hardest part was always getting out of the car. Always.

My heart felt like it was about to burst out of my chest at any moment. My eyes burned from tears I wouldn't let fall. The sudden feeling of suffocation made me close my eyes. After I counted back from ten, I took a deep breath and exhaled quietly. I opened my eyes when I felt a pull on my hand, and then a soft kiss on the back of it.

"You a'ight?" I looked over at Santonio.

Hell no, I wasn't *a'ight*. But he knew that. He was just trying to be there, and I appreciated him for that. "Yeah, I'm okay." I smiled.

"You ready?" he asked.

I looked back out of my window. "No."

I only came to Jeanette's gravesite twice a year—the day she was born and the day she died. Other than those two days, I avoided the cemetery all together. She'd been gone for four years. She would've been twenty-nine today. My best friend, my sister, my confidante...my muthafuckin dawg.

When I was here, both the good and bad ate at me. The times we skipped school just to go to the mall, snuck out of the house to hang with the corner boys, went clubbing, or had adult sleepers with Skyy and Sasha just to catch up with one another. To the hard times— when we argued, fought, went weeks without speaking, or flat out disregarded one another's feelings. The good always outweighed the bad, though. We shared more laughs than arguments, so I won't lie and say that didn't help me through each visit.

I opened my door and Santonio followed suit. After shutting our doors, we met in front my Chrysler 300 and reached out for one another. Hand in hand, we walked towards Jeanette's headstone. Santonio gave my hand a small squeeze, and I gripped his hand back as a silent thank you. As we got nearer, my vision blurred.

We stopped a few feet away and I released Santonio's hand. He stayed put as I approached her with a heavy heart. The pictures of her, Kory Jr., some family, and a few friends on her headstone made me smile a little. The flowers surrounding it looked to be brand new. This was the first year I hadn't brought balloons. I just didn't see the point anymore.

Going into a squatting position, I ran my hand across a photo of her. The first tear slid down my cheek, and a sniffle followed. I stared silently at her, wishing shit was different. This shit never got easier. As a matter of fact, each year got much worse.

"Nette..." I sighed. "Happy birthday. I wish you were here to cele-brate wit' us. I can't believe your ass is almost thirty." I chuckled. "Old ass." I paused to wipe my face. "I didn't bring balloons this time. But I got a bottle at home and every shot I take is for you." The rain picked up a little reminding me I had left my umbrella in the car. "I tried to call your mom to talk to KJ, but she ain't fuckin' with me at all. I know she's mad at me."

When Jeanette first went missing, Ma Williams, Jeanette's mother, had asked me if I knew Santonio. I lied and told her no. When she found out he was Sanaa's daddy, she didn't yell at me or scold me.

Instead, she she shook her head in disappointment and cut me off. She went from letting me FaceTime KJ to not even responding to my text messages whenever I asked about him.

"Nette..." I paused. "I took Santonio back, and we're getting married. Don't be mad at me. I really love him. Despite his flaws, I know he loves me too." The rain drops got bigger, reminding me I had to wrap this visit up. I usually stayed longer but I didn't want to get sick.

I stood up, placed my hand on the top of her headstone, and closed my eyes.

"Dear God, sometimes I question You. I just try to understand some of Your reasoning. I trust You, though. And I know You got Jeanette regardless of what she did because You knew her heart. Please help Ma Williams find it in her heart to forgive and continue to watch over KJ. He's a kid growing up without a mother and father. I know he's lost." I opened my eyes and took a step back. "Amen."

# TONE

The ride home from the cemetery was quiet. I knew E was in her feelings because today was Jeanette's birthday. She had woken up with a bad attitude and stayed cooped up in our bedroom damn near the whole morning and afternoon. Finally, around three-thirty, she came stomping down the stairs with her coat and purse in hand and sunglasses on her face. I was gon' leave her alone until she snapped on me and told me to leave her alone.

I yoked her little ass up and bear hugged her until she whined for me to let her go. Then, I asked to ride out with her. I saw how emotional she got at the graveyard; it took her a few minutes just to get out of the car. I knew her homegirl's death took a toll on her, but it was the first time I saw just how much it affected her. I reached over and rubbed her thigh.

"You hungry?"

She shook her head.

"Well, I am." Erin looked over at me and mugged the fuck out me. I tried to not to laugh at her mean ass, so I quickly faced my window.

"What do you want to eat?" she asked with an attitude.

"Go to Jack Stacks." I informed her while going through my phone.

"Santonio, can you get it to go?" She removed some of the bass out of her tone. "I'm not in the mood to be in a room full of people."

"I got you."

We didn't exchange any more words after that. Some chick who she said was "Nao" seeped from the speakers. When we pulled into Jack Stack's, the parking lot was full. Erin turned the music down and sucked her teeth as she tried to find an empty spot.

"Can you just run in there real quick?" She stopped in front of the door and put the car in park. "I'm tired."

"Man, get out. You need to put something on your stomach." I opened my door and got out. As I waited for Erin, Royal walked out of the restaurant.

"What's good boss man?"

"Sup youngin'." I walked around to Erin's side and pulled her door open. "Get out."

She smacked her lips and said a few inaudible curse words but didn't get out.

I gently grabbed a hold of her forearm and helped her out. I then opened the back door, removed her purse and handed it to her. "Let's go." I grabbed a hold of her hand.

"I told you I wasn't hungry." Erin grumbled but latched onto my hand as we walked into the restaurant.

"Party for two?" the hostess asked with a smile on her face.

"Yeah."

"No."

Me and Erin answered at the same time.

The hostess looked back and forth between us, a confused expression gracing her face.

"Two." I informed her as I gripped Erin's hand tighter.

She huffed. "Santonio, my clothes are damp, and I know my hair looks crazy."

I looked over and down at her. "It's warm in here, your clothes will dry, and yo hair looks fine." I examined the bun on the top of her head. When we first left the house it looked slicker, but now it was curly. My baby still looked flyy to me, so I didn't see the problem.

We followed the hostess to the back of the restaurant and when we cut the corner, Rome and Erica damn near ran into us.

"Bout time y'all got here." Erica smiled at Erin. "I was just about to call you."

Erin looked up at me, confused.

Rome hooked her arm into Erin's other arm. "I'm happy you finally came out that room, sis. You look cute."

Erica nodded in agreement.

The hostess led us to the party room and pushed the door open. When we stepped inside, the room was packed full of people talking, laughing, and eating. Sanaa rushed towards us, cheesing.

"Hi, Mommy." She held her arms up for Erin.

Rome and Erica walked off and Erin picked Sanaa up. "Hey, Naa-Naa." She nuzzled her lovingly. "I missed you today." Erin looked around the room at everybody and then back to me. "What is this? Why are Eli and Sasha here?" She frowned.

"They know not be on no bullshit and it's a birthday party." I shrugged walking off to get something to eat and she followed me. The cake on the table had huge picture of Jeanette on it a few candles.

"A wha—" E stopped midsentence and put Sanaa down.

"Auntie Erin!" A little voice made me and her turn around. "Auntie!" KJ ran full speed in our direction with a snaggle-toothed smile.

Erin walked quickly to meet him halfway and they shared a long embrace. I watched as she knelt down, laughing and she inspected him. KJ grinned, nodding his head at whatever she was saying before wrapping his arms around her neck. Skyy walked up to them with Jeanette's mama, Ms. Williams, with a wide smile spread across her face as well. Erin stood up and they exchanged a few words before she turned around to look at me.

I smirked as her watery eyes danced around me.

I wasn't the perfect nigga, but I knew what I had at home. I had a down ass chick who loved me unconditionally. She was patient, strong, smart as fuck, and despite of her upbringing, a devoted mother. Not mention sexy than a muthafucka. And she was about to be my wife.

We had been through a whole bunch of bullshit, but it made our bond stronger. Made me realize I couldn't live without her. Had me wanting to be a better man for her and my family. I would do anything to make her life easier if it meant keeping a smile on her pretty face. Even if I'd had to beg Ms. Williams to bring KJ down for Jeanette's birthday when I was in Minneapolis to get Rome.

That was another reason I needed to get to Minnesota right after the New Year. After cashing Ms. Williams out and promising to keep KJ safe, she not only agreed to come down for her birthday, but she agreed to let KJ spend the summers down here too. I knew how much he meant to Erin because he was the only thing left of Jeanette.

The room got louder, but Erin's gaze never left mine. A small side smile tugged at her lips and she shook her head.

I nodded knowingly before turning around to finish making my plate.

# EPILOGUE

**If life is a movie, then you're the best part.**

ERIN SURFED through her Louis Vuitton suitcase in a frustrated manner. She could've sworn she had brought her swimsuit. Tone was already dressed and waiting on her, calling out for her to "Hurry up" every few minutes. She grabbed her other bag and unzipped it, cursing out loud. She didn't understand why she hadn't come across it yet.

Erin specifically asked Erica to toss it in a bag when she and Rome were helping her pack. She snatched up her phone and scrolled through her call log. Pressing on Erica's name, Erin pressed the phone to her ear and looked up at the vaulted ceiling. She tapped her long, coffin shaped nails impatiently as she waited for her little sister to pick up. When Erica did, she was laughing at something Rome was saying.

"What's up, E?"

"What are y'all doing? Where's Sanaa and Toni?" Erin sighed. She could hear her oldest daughter saying something but couldn't quite understand.

Erica rolled her eyes. "We're getting ready to go to a slumber party. Chance invited us. Why aren't you somewhere having sex?"

"Erica!" Erin frowned. Her little sister was growing up and every day she got more outspoken and ornery, especially since she'd started hanging around Rome. "I'm not about to talk about my sex life with you."

Erica laughed and put the phone on speaker. "Sanaa, your mom is on the phone."

"Hi, Mommy." Sanaa wasted no time jumping on the phone. She was a daddy's girl, but to her, mommy was the ultimate being. If Tone was her Superman, then Erin was her Wonder Woman.

"Hey, Naa-Naa. I miss you," Erin cooed.

"I miss you too."

"Erin, why are you calling?" Rome jumped in on the conversation. "I just talked to Tonio not too long ago. I thought y'all were going swimming."

"We are. Erica, I thought you packed my swimsuit." Erin double checked her luggage. "I don't see it."

"When you gave it to me, I handed it to Rome and told her to put it in your bag."

Erin's heart dropped. Rome was a forgetful weed head. You could tell her to check the oven in two minutes, and in thirty, the kitchen was clouded with smoke. Erin didn't understand how Rome could be so high the entire day. But somehow, her sister-in-love got through each day completely faded.

Erin knew Rome was going through a lot; she'd moved to a whole new state with a group of people she'd just met. She stayed to herself a lot, Erin noticed too. She usually didn't leave the house unless Erica dragged her to the mall, or to an occasional movie. Rome and Erica had become really close over the past couple weeks, and it caught Erin by surprise because they were nothing alike. Erica was a loud spoiled brat, and Rome was a quiet stoner.

"Ask Rome which bag she put it in." Erin closed her eyes.

"Ro Ro, did you pack Erin's swimsuit?"

Erin waited for a response as the line grew eerily quiet.

"E, she said she put it on your bag."

Erin rolled her eyes. "Okay, bye." She ended the call and stood up. Now she was going to have to ask Tone to take her to get some new swimwear.

"Why you ain't dressed?" He looked up from his phone.

"I should've doubled checked my bags before we left. Rome and Erica helped me pack."

Tone chuckled knowingly. He'd been living in a house with those two for almost a month. Erica was moody and Rome was forgetful. The two combined was a recipe for disaster.

"It's cool." He shrugged. "I wasn't trying to go swimming anyway."

The couple had been in Greece for three days now. The first day and half was them catching up on sleep. The second day, they'd sexed each other back into a coma. The house they were staying in had an indoor pool and jacuzzi, and Erin had finally talked Tone into hopping in. She approached him pulling her tank top over her head.

"We can skinny dip." She smirked.

Tone lustfully looked his fiancé over. Erin was almost too perfect in his eyes. "We might as well get in the shower then." He figured they wouldn't be in the pool long before he was slamming her down on the dick. They could kill two birds with one stone if they had shower sex instead.

Erin laughed at the devilish grin on his face. "Never mind, nasty." She hopped onto the bed and sat cross-legged. "Let's find something to do." She reached for her iPad. "Wanna eat first?"

Tone's mind went straight to the gutter.

"*Food?*" Erin snickered while searching the web. "What kind of food do you wanna try?"

"Don't matter." He shrugged. They had a personal chef in the house, he didn't understand why Erin wanted to leave. They were going to be in Greece for two weeks; Tone figured that would just enough time to keep Erin locked up long enough to get pregnant.

They sat silently as Erin made reservations online.

"What time is it?" Tone asked, lying on his back with his eyes closed.

"Uhh...1:45pm." Erin finalized their dinner plans. "So, get dressed, reservation is at five." She looked him over slowly.

"I know what I wanna do now." Tone spoke.

"I already made reservations and I'm hungry."

"We can eat afterward. Shit we can celebrate til the sun comes up tomorrow."

Erin gave him the side-eye. "And what are we celebrating?" She silently prayed he hadn't come across the positive pregnancy test she planned on surprising him with. She tried to remember if she asked him to go in her bags for anything.

She'd taken the test their first night in Greece. Tone had been sleep, so once she got the results, she wrapped the test up, put it back in the box, and hid it in the front compartment of her bag. Tone's birthday was in two days, and she wanted to tell him then.

"Let's go get married."

Erin tilted her head slightly. Had she heard him right? "Married? When? Now? In Greece?" Erin rambled off each question.

"Yeah."

"But our family isn't here." Erin's heart felt like it was about to burst out of her chest. She didn't know if the palpitating was from excitement or fear. "It's cold outside, the weather's not even right for a wedding." It was Tone's idea to come to Greece because he had never been, and around his birthday was the only free time he had to leave the country unless it was business related.

"So what?" He stared into her eyes. "I wanna marry you today."

Erin jumped off the bed and rushed back into the closet without saying a word. Tone frowned as he waited for her to come back out. Just when he was about to go after her, Erin ambled out, slipping her arms into her coat. She then walked past him and towards the door, securing her hands in her gloves. When she saw Tone hadn't moved from his position in the bed, Erin stopped in her tracks, turned around and faced him.

"Put your shoes on and come on." She smiled. "Let's go get married."

# THE END

Want to be notified when the new, hot Urban Fiction and Interracial Romance books are released? Text the keyword "JWP" to 22828 to receive an email notifying you of new releases, giveaways, announcements, and more!

Jessica Watkins Presents is currently accepting submissions for the following genres: Urban Romance, Interracial Romance, and Interracial Romance/Paranormal. If you are interested in becoming a best selling author and have a complete manuscript, please send the synopsis and the first three chapters to jwp.submissions@gmail.com.

Made in the USA
Middletown, DE
02 December 2021